CW0521240

Gwen grew up in the Yorkshire and enjoyed life with her animals; ponies and later on horses were a big part of her life but she also enjoyed fast cars. Eventually, with her second husband, she moved to Scotland and felt totally at home. The lochs and mountains became a part of everyday life and on the very rare occasions she had to go into the city, she could not wait to get on the ferry and back to the relative peace and quiet of Argyll.

I would like to dedicate this book to my husband, Paul; our children, Guy and Louise; our wonderful grandchildren, Sophie, Alfie and Layla; and our son-in-law, Andy.

Gwen Ineson

TRAIGH

AUSTIN MACAULEY PUBLISHERS™

LONDON • CAMBRIDGE • NEW YORK • SHARJAH

ISBN 9781528903622 (Paperback)
ISBN 9781528903639 (Hardback)
ISBN 9781528957496 (ePub e-book)

www.austinmacauley.com

First Published (2019)
Austin Macauley Publishers Ltd
25 Canada Square
Canary Wharf
London
E14 5LQ

Enormous thanks must go to my sister, Sue; and her husband, Geoff, if they hadn't kept all the letters, I couldn't have written this.

Hello, my name is...actually I don't have one yet, I've just been born. It's the 6th of December and I am in Forfar in Angus, Scotland.

I can't tell you much, I'm too young to remember, but I was told my mother was called Kate and my father was called Cadbury, both working sheepdogs. I remember being in an area that was overgrown with pipes and logs and it was a great playground for me and my brothers and sisters, far better than being in a kennel.

One day a couple came to look for a new pup and that's when I got my name which is Traigh. (Pronounced Try.) Traigh is a village between Arisaig and Mallaig on the western coast of Scotland and also I am Tri coloured, so they chose well.

Hi, we are Traigh's friends, (Paul and Gwen) some folk would say owners, but we never owned him; we just all belonged to each other.

We had decided it was time to have another dog, we were open minded as to a dog or a bitch, we just knew it must be a border collie. Even though the dreadful Foot and Mouth outbreak was well past, we found farmers were not breeding and we soon realised this was going to be much harder than we thought.

We lived at St Catherine's, overlooking Loch Fyne, surrounded by sheep and highland cattle so we thought getting a dog would be a doddle. Eventually after ringing local vets, we rang a vet up in Fort William and they knew a lady who had some pups, but after a conversation with her we realised they were show dogs, fine boned, probably not up to the mountainous countryside we lived in.

We started looking and asking around again, eventually a vet rang to say a Mr Ian Gray up at Forfar had some pups and gave us his number. We made an appointment and set off, we remember it snowed heavily all the way there and once or twice we even thought of turning back, but that might mean we missed the perfect pup.

We arrived and was shown the large area that the pups were in, we had always said unless we choose the same pup we would come away without one.

The pups all scampered over to the gate and wanted to be made a great fuss of, except one, this pup sat on a boulder and watched us and we watched him. The draw was there immediately. Ian Gray went to get him, he passed him to Paul and that was it, we both knew straight away this was the one.

We paid for him and started for home with the best friend we have ever had.

Traigh had been with us for a week and I decided to write to my sister Sue, but do it through Traigh's eyes, I thought it would make her laugh and then started correspondence that went on for years. This is his very first letter...

Chapter 1

Dear Sue and Geoff,

Gwen thought I should write to you, I have absolutely no idea why as I don't know who you are but she says I can tell you anything I want, she might regret that!

Day 1

Well now there I was just minding my own business when...well I'd better go back a bit now I know the story.

This couple called Paul and Gwen were looking for a puppy, not just any puppy, a sheepdog puppy and to cut a long story short they were told of a man who bred 'Woodsmoke' dogs who lived in Forfar, apparently Paul said, "How bloody far?"

Anyway there I was minding my own business playing in the pen with my brothers and sisters when along came this couple and stared at us over the meshing, bit of a cheek if you ask me, they didn't even ask if we minded, for some reason they liked me the best, well actually it's not surprising, I am rather handsome. They said, "He's okay." I was shattered, okay...just okay. Come on now I'm brilliant my mum said so, anyway they decided to have me, huh! I didn't have a say in it at all. They had been to look at my mum and my uncle, I expect to ask permission seeing as Dad was working.

Now I have to say I wasn't so sure, I thought she was a bit dodgy, she came into the pen all nice and clean and came out filthy and she didn't seem to mind a bit, definitely strange.

Shortly after this I get put into this thing called a car, the man who was called Paul made this car go and he kept looking round, he said I was cute, handsome yes, cute no. I decided to get my own back on them so I was sick all over the one called Gwen, wow she stunk.

We stopped in Perth and they bought me bowls, a bed, some toys and a collar and lead and different food to what I had been having, but Mr Gray had given them some of the food I was used to, so I could get introduced to the new food slowly and not have a tummy upset.

We arrived back at my new home, it's a funny place, apparently I am going to live INSIDE, I kept looking for the straw but I have this new squashy bed. Seeing as both Gwen and I stunk we had to have a shower, I loved it when Paul dried me with a big towel. It was great fun.

I had a bit of tea and then we all went for a short walk and I was attached to this silly thing called a lead, but it was okay, I think it made them feel secure .We were on this thing called a shore which had lots of moving water that tasted awful, strange things in the sky that sounded like the farm cat but Gwen told me they were seagulls.

We went back home and I fell asleep on my new bed, oh boy it was so comfy, I needed to go out in the night but I was a good boy and very quick and I went straight back to sleep.

Day 2.
Straight outside, good idea but they could let an important puppy like me wake up a bit first. Breakfast was good, I was hungry. Paul went away to do something called work, Gwen did a few chores and then we went for a walk attached to that silly thing again, we went into the woods and I soon found out that when she calls and pats her leg, if I go running back to her she gives me this tiny biscuit and a good pat, so I often run back to her even if she hasn't asked me to.

I had an easy day we went for lots of little walks. Paul came home and played with me, actually he plays with me more than Gwen, she's a bit bossy, but I'll get her trained in time. I was glad when it was time for bed, I was tired, but I did remember to get her up at 3.00am, serves her right for being bossy.

Day 3.

Its Saturday and Paul stayed here today, Gwen put me in the car and drove me to the shore, we could walk it in no time at all but she says I have to get used to it, anyway to show my annoyance I barked as loudly as I could all the way there and back, it had no effect at all, I think she must be deaf. I spent the morning helping Paul, it was good fun.

A nice lady told Gwen of a forestry track so we went to have a look, over to the end of the Park, through a couple of fields and then oh heaven. A long wide track that goes way up into the hills, I ran on ahead and when I turned around I couldn't see Gwen, I was really scared and started to shake, then moments later she appeared, I raced back to her and was made a big fuss of, it was so good to see her and I decided never to go too far in front again.

Paul and I went up the track again later in the evening, I was now getting tired and was ready for my bed.

Day 4.

I, thought us youngsters were allowed to have a lie in on a Sunday, no chance of that here, I was back in the car and driven down to the shore, I didn't bark on the way back, it seems like a waste of energy if she's deaf.

After breakfast I helped Paul fit a new carpet in Gwen's office, I kept moving things out of his way as I didn't want him to kneel on them and hurt himself, I think I must have been a very good assistant as after a while Gwen took me for a little walk, I think it was to say thank you.

Later in the day, Duncan from Lochgoilhead came over to see us, I think he was very impressed with me, mind you I was on my very best behaviour, having said that, 'Bossy Boots Gwen' was there, so I had to be.

Paul asked if I wanted to go to Inverary with him, but I didn't so I pretended to be asleep, but then Gwen was busy so I wished I had said yes.

Once again a busy day and I am tired, I do hope Gwen doesn't wake me up going to the bathroom tonight, it is most inconsiderate of her, seeing as I have stopped needing to going out in the night.

Day 5
I went to Lochgoilhead today with Gwen, it's a lovely place although I was a bit too tired to take it all in, Gwen and I had been for a good walk and it was a bit steep, Gwen used a stick to help her, but I expect it's hard only having two legs.

There are these enormous dogs up in the hills with twigs on their heads, Gwen says I am just being silly, they are Red Deer, but how would I know I haven't been to school. I hope I don't grow so big because people EAT them.

Day 6
I didn't like today, she kept getting me wet, it rained hard all day and she kept dragging me out, I should not have to go out in such dreadful weather. A man came and put in a machine that sometimes rings, I wanted to help but Gwen wouldn't let me. Paul came home and they took me to the Vets, I didn't know what it was, but I didn't really like it too much so I not going to discuss it, but I will say I didn't make a fuss. I was confused though because this lady let me stand on her table and I'm not allowed to do that at home, I don't like these dual standards. I was glad when the day was over.

Day 7
Today the weather was so wild that the water was right up on the shore and I couldn't even have a little paddle. It completely spoilt my routine so I hid a sock under one of the seats and kept having a quick play with it when no one was looking. It didn't last long, old hawk eye misses nothing and she took it off me.

I learned to sit and lie down this week but I don't really know why I have to do it when she says, she would not do it if I asked her, but she says I ask too many questions.

Also I have been thinking about the car, I am going to stop barking and making a fuss, I am 13 weeks old now and it makes me look like a baby.

Well that's my first week over with them and it's been alright, I have decided to stay but I wrote this account so that in the future when perhaps I am not so good as I am now, I can call on you as witnesses.

If I become spoilt then it's down to Paul and Gwen, because I have been very good to start with, so if you don't mind I'd like you to keep this in a safe place.

Very best wishes,
Traigh

I am a great believer in dogs being treated as dogs and not small humans, so he was not allowed on furniture, not allowed in the bedroom, not to sit by the table and not to be given lots and lots of titbits and treats, which usually make dogs ill, especially chocolate which can be fatal.

Training started immediately, I can't whistle so we taught him to look at hand signals as well as the spoken voice.

It took two weeks to teach him to sit, stay, lie down, wait, come back and to go in whichever direction we pointed. I would initially give him a tiny treat and a good pat, after a week, the treats stopped and a pat and kind word was his reward. As a youngster we went through these few commands two or three times a day and they stayed with him forever.

Paul and I worked on two caravan parks and Traigh was with us every day. With sheep everywhere we had to be sure he wasn't going to be a problem. I walked him with a twig in my hand and if he looked in the direction of sheep I would tap him gently on the nose and say no, again his intelligence told him he had not to take any notice of them.

For a few weeks he stayed with me at St Catherine's, then I also went to work at the Park in Lochgoilhead. Paul made Traigh a kennel opposite my office and he was told not to go off the slabs that were in front of it, he never did, he was never tied up, he didn't need to be and if the weather was nice he used to sit on the roof and watch the world go by. He wasn't there all day, I was always going to check something on the Park so he was with me or away with Paul in his van.

Paul used to go up the hill behind the Park every morning to check the water supply, he would go through the sheep gate and let Traigh out and he would race over the hill side, ignoring any sheep and be waiting at the top as Paul bumped his van slowly over the rough track, a breather as Paul checked the supply and then Paul would say "okay, see you at the gate" and that was Traigh's signal to race back down again and wait for Paul with his tail wagging and his tongue hanging out.

It was around this time, early on, that he started to undo the laces on Paul's work boots every night, he never chewed them, just left them at the side of Paul's boots and Paul had to re-thread his boots every morning, we never worked out why and then one morning the laces hadn't been touched and he never did it again. This routine of his lasted 8 months.

Chapter 2

Dear Sue Geoff,

Now since I wrote that first account to you I also distributed it to some of my canine friends they have been begging me to keep on writing. They appreciate the humans being put in their place occasionally. I have to agree, whilst you humans think you own us, do you? I'm not sure, you can be quite strange. Think about it, if we have to go to the vets, you humans get all emotional and often cry, but do we when you go to the doctors? Point made, I believe.

Right then, well after my first week things began to settle down and get some normality to it, that's if you can stretch your imagination and call either Paul or Gwen normal, no I didn't think so.

I wake at 6.30am, Gwen takes me out for a quick puddle, I have my breakfast and then I have to wait until Paul goes to work at 7.30am. Gwen puts on her wellies (it's usually raining) and we go for a walk, by the fourth corner Paul has rung to say he's at work, its rather pathetic, its only about 7 miles away. There are rabbits about and I make a pretence of giving chase, after two or three seconds I give up, I don't see the point, I don't need to catch my own food. We sometimes see deer but I am a bit scared of them, they are so big and seem to leap in the air, I don't want one of them landing on top of me, I would get squashed.

After about an hour we go back and it's time for work. I help as much as I can but really my role is more of a carer, someone has to look out for her and of course she consults me on everything. We have some very in depth conversations but they are often one sided, I do believe it comes from good parentage and of course I am a true Scot, where as she was born south of the Border.

We go for another walk in the afternoon and then Paul takes me again when he comes home, we go down to the shore and I often come home soaking wet and if I am really quick I can rush in and shake myself next to Gwen. She thinks I do it on purpose and of course I do, its good clean fun, well not always clean depending on what I have rolled in. In between these walks if I need to have a puddle, I just need to ask, Gwen is coming along very nicely. I'll have her trained in no time.

Whilst the above is an average day, lots of other things happen to make the days more interesting.

Paul was painting the balcony to the office and he had put the paint tin lid on the deck. Gwen asked him to move it as I would no doubt put my nose in it, so he put it on the grass just below the balcony. Now you do have to realise I did not do this on purpose but I came racing round the corner, could not stop and slid under the bottom rail of this balcony and yes, straight onto the paint tin lid. I was absolutely covered in green paint.

Gwen took me in to get me clean, to avoid getting herself even more covered in paint she stripped off and put me in the shower. I stood so patiently in the shower whilst Gwen had to answer the door wrapped in a towel, covered in green paint to find a lady at the door asking if she could say hello to "that sweet little puppy". I heard Gwen being ever so polite but I bet it was through gritted teeth. Anyway Paul thought it was funny and so did I.

Paul fitted me a carpet in the back of the car but took it for granted that I would like the colour, it was purple, I ask you PURPLE. I kept trying to get rid of it and pushed it out of the car when I was getting in and out. It was enough to give you car sickness, apparently it was an off cut, fancy giving me leftovers, I can tell you I was really insulted. After a while he got the message and I got a nice restful beige one.

The car is fine, but Paul's van is something else, it was designed by aliens, it has plastic seats and Paul expects me to sit on them. Freezing in winter and burn your bum in summer. Sorry but not for me, standards and all that.

It's been nice and warm lately, the sun has made shadows on the floor which I don't really understand, I keep chasing them, its great fun. Gwen put some ice cubes in my water bowl to keep it cool. I didn't like them. It's just not every day you see UFO's (Unidentified Floating Objects). She said they were fine but I was not sure at all, but after a while I plucked up the courage to have a look and they had GONE, just disappeared, vanished completely. Maybe we have a ghost or a witch, if it is a witch I bet it's called Gwen.

The other day Gwen got lots of heather plants to put round the office, they were sitting quite inoffensively in their pots with little plastic labels so I thought I would be helpful and collect all the labels for her, I did leave them in quite a neat pile, but now she doesn't know which is which. I'll make it up to her, when she's ready to plant them, I'll dig the holes, I'm good at that.

Gwen is beginning to doubt my parentage because I keep complaining about the midges, she says if I am a true Scot then I should be used to them, I cannot see how my ancestry would give me immunity, although I am nearly Royal, well the Queen passes by where I was born on her way to Balmoral, that counts doesn't it.

The midges don't seem to bother Paul too much but they eat Gwen alive, they think the dinner gong has gone when she goes outside, even I feel a bit sorry for her. She looks like Blobby, all covered in spots, she's getting fat as well, perhaps I shouldn't have said that, it was a bit below the belt, actually that's where the fat is.

Oh dear, I think I am becoming a little sarcastic, I get it from Paul, Gwen says he's got a degree in it, anyway I'll try not to be. I'll write (or dictate) again soon, take care.

The Management (They only think they are)

As you can see life with Traigh was good, evenings would find us usually on the shore and Traigh loved to chase

19

the waves but he wasn't too fond of going right into the water, we knew this had to be overcome as we were surrounded by Lochs and Rivers.

On our next day off we headed to Ostell Bay, a hidden gem of place, golden sand and water that went out a long way before it became deep. We were told there was absolutely no amenities there, so we took a picnic, golf umbrella for Traigh to go under if it became too hot, fresh water and bowl for him, we were laden down with things.

We had taken his favourite ball and Paul and Traigh headed for the water, Paul threw the ball at first and slowly, very slowly Traigh went a bit further than a paddle. Paul kept walking up and down the shoreline getting a little deeper bit by bit, then without Traigh realising it he was swimming. Since then at every opportunity he would be in the water. As the years went by I would often see both Paul and Traigh in the sea swimming side by side.

One day I was fishing off the pier, Traigh was playing on the shore, but he suddenly decided to come back, but too quickly, the pier was slippery and he couldn't stop at the end.

He looked like a cartoon dog trying to back pedal, anyway he went straight off the end and landed in the water with a big splash. Completely unperturbed he swam back to the shore and was fine. I was very glad he could swim though.

Chapter 3

Dear Sue and Geoff,

Not a lot has happened since the last letter, I have been to the Kennels a couple of times, just for the afternoon, they said it was so I would be okay when they left me for longer, but I know it was so they could go to the George in Inverary for lunch. There are other dogs at the kennels, but some of them are a bit stupid, they bark for no apparent reason.

I got into trouble yesterday, Gwen and I went to Carrick at lunchtime for a walk and I swam over to some rocks to a colony of seals and they all jumped into the water, hang on, it gets worse, I jumped in after them. Gwen was not a happy bunny, she said I would catch my death of cold, numpty, she should know I'm waterproof, but I was a bit smelly. She told me off, or stared me off, she doesn't speak it's just the way she looks it's enough to make my pads curl. I definitely will not do that again and I was really good for the rest of the day.

It's the Christmas Party next week, we are staying overnight in a holiday home in Kingfisher village over at Lochgoilhead, I said I wasn't going unless I got an invite, but I needn't have worried mine came first. Gwen asked if it was long frock and Tiara do, it's not, so she'll probably go in her wellies. If she wore a dress folk would think Paul had another woman. I shall wear my best collar and having a natural ruff, I won't need a dickie bow.

I have said I am definitely not dancing if they play 'Who Put the Dogs Out'.

I'll say goodbye for now and make sure Gwen gets well wrapped up before we go out, the wind gives her earache. She gets earache with the wind, I just get it from her, as for the wind well...

Take care,
Traigh

Now my Sister Sue and husband Geoff were looking forward to Traigh's correspondence and lots of their friends were reading it too, unbeknown to us he was getting quite a following.

Traigh was never a naughty puppy (a little mischievous occasionally) but never naughty, I always maintain that any dog that has enough exercise will not be a chewer or a destroyer of things, by the time bedtime comes they should be ready for sleep.

Traigh had a toybox and we could ask him to pass us certain toys, like the penguin, teddy bear or ball etc....although he had lots of toys he always knew which was which.

At ten o'clock, Paul would put the kettle on for a cup of tea, I would take Traigh out for a few minutes, then he would be asked to "put your toys away" and he would pick them up one by one and put them back in the box and go to his bed.

One evening the 'mischief' came out, it was about 2.30am and I heard a squeak, I got up to find Traigh playing with a plastic rabbit that had a squeak inside. I gave him 'the look' and he slowly picked it up, put it back in the box, returned to his bed laid down and crossed his paws and put his head on them. Not a word was spoken, he never played with his toys at night again, but we came to realise over time that when he crossed his paws he was fed up.

Chapter 4

Hello,

Guess what those two numpties of mine have done now?

They booked to go and see Phantom of the Opera, they didn't read it properly because it was Phantom AND the Opera. They got there before they realised their mistake, it was two people on pianos with a guy on a drum and three folk singing.

The 'Theatre' was a hall with rows of seats like at school and badminton courts marking the floor. There was an unusual array of people coming in, a farmer in the front row had on a very nice suit but had forgotten to take off his farm boots. One lady had on a very snazzy gold top, she looked very overdressed and then seated behind Paul was a man who had on a captains hat and looked like Popeye, his pal looked at least 100yrs old and hummed all the way through, totally out of tune.

Anyway they had to make the most of it, everyone eagerly looked to the front, the curtain didn't go up, they didn't have one. On walked the musicians to polite applause and then on came Maria Kessleman who had played opposite Michael Crawford in Phantom down in London, she then proceeded to sing a medley from Les Miserable. They looked at each other and tried really hard not to laugh.

Two more singers came on and they occasionally addressed the audience and sang songs from the last 100yrs. They said after Act 1 there would be an interval. Now I would be getting confused here as there was no acting at all, anyway the interval arrived and you could get, tea, coffee or alcohol from a very tiny bar, you could tell the ones that didn't get out much, they were first in the queue.

Paul and Gwen said 'Act 2' was quite enjoyable, the audience were invited to sing along, but us Scots can be quite shy at times so not a voice was heard, but there was plenty of foot tapping and most of it in rhythm.

I enjoyed them telling me all about it when they got home which was about 10.30pm, they are allowed to stay out until then occasionally, it can't all be about me.

Although talking of me, I have decided that just being called Traigh is just not enough, so I am going to be HRH Traigh. His Royal Hound.

So it's goodbye from me for now.
HRH Traigh.
(P.S. I do hope the other HRH doesn't mind.)

Around this time Traigh started going to the kennels a little more, we had built it up slowly so that he would never be stressed at going, but Traigh being Traigh was so laid back and easy going it was never a problem. Jane who had the kennels at the time didn't like sheepdogs as pets and thought they should only be working animals, she did have the good grace to say he was an exception and so easy to have in the kennels, but again this was down to always being busy and not bored.

Chapter 5

Hi, hope you are both okay,

I asked Gwen to type this as I am very busy helping Paul rack out his van and I need to supervise or he'll make a dogs dinner out of it.

This week we all went to Glasgow to B & Q, I'm not sure which is worse Glasgow or B & Q. It's all concrete, hardly any grass and not a mountain to be seen. Lots of people live in flats, but they are not flat at all. They are piled on top of each other like boxes that are stacked up. They should call them boxes, you humans have some funny names for things.

Paul and I had a disagreement this week, you see when I watch the telly, I get a crick in my neck from looking up at the screen, he doesn't because he sits on the sofa, yet I can't. I have put in a job request for a small pedestal to be made for me in front of the telly, but I saw him file it in the bin. YET, when he needs my help and I have to go with him, then I am allowed to sit on the seat of his van.

HMS Argyll was in Loch Fyne over the weekend. They (the crew or whatever you call them) were there to exercise their right to freedom of the Town. (Inverary) They were to march down the High Street with the pipe band, have a ceremony on the green and in the evening have dinner with the Duke and Duchess. I think perhaps rain stopped play, it poured down. Pity I was going to offer to be night watchdog and look after their nice boat, it's a really big one, but it's not finished as it is grey, the colour of undercoat.

I forgot to tell you we have bought a piece of land over on the Island of Isla. Actually it's a bit of a joke. Gwen bought Paul a bottle of Laphroaig whisky and you could join the 'Friends of Isla Whisky group', so now we own one square foot of land on Isla. To keep the ownership we have to visit once a year and have a dram at the distillery, good marketing I thought. They have a pal who is into one upmanship, so they are waiting for the right moment to tell him they are landowners, but they are not going to tell him straight away how big it is. I can't wait to see his face.

Paul and I are on our own on Wednesday night as Gwen is going on a course down in Lancaster, its Paul's birthday so I'll have to woof a few bars of happy birthday, if I nod my head from side to side he'll think I'm Stevie Wonder.

I watched a bit of Crufts last week, crikey there are some sights there, they should get a life and do a proper days' work and build up some muscles. Mark my words they will all succumb to heart attacks, a good days work never did a dog any harm. Having said that Gwen is getting on a bit, she can't do what she used to, 10 miles hard walking and she's shattered. If my maths is right and I was told the right information, I have worked out that in dog years I think she is 343 years old. I not sure even Jesus lived that long, I think she must have known his dad because she is always saying "Oh my god".

Oh! I nearly forgot, we went up to Ben Nevis and went up in the cable car to the restaurant. Gwen's not good with heights as you know, so she sat on the floor with me and pretended that I might be scared of the cable car swaying. Who is she kidding? She just didn't want to look over the side and used me as an excuse. I don't mind helping out but she could have asked. She could join me on the floor but there is no way I would have been allowed to join them on the seat which I find very unfair as I think I would have liked the view.

We have some Highland cattle in the field. This may not be true but I was told that if the horns point up they are female and if they point down they are male. There is one that has one horn up and one horn down. Paul calls it Jessie.

Oh well, must go, take care.
HRH Traigh.

The summer passed by nicely and autumn turned slowly towards winter.

Traigh was 2 years old and life was pretty good.

I worked over at Lochgoilhead pretty much full time, only occasionally staying at St Catherine's but Paul would always be at St. Catherine's on a Sunday, (providing there was not an emergency at Lochgoilhead), so Traigh stayed with Paul on Sundays.

A lovely lady called Trisha who was originally frightened of dogs started to take an interest in Traigh and regularly took him for a walk, she adored him and they enjoyed each other's company a lot.

At this time we had a touring caravan which was sited down at Ardlamont, we didn't use it much as we lived in a place that was just as beautiful, but when we did, we used to collect muscles on the shore and they were massive hence his next letter.

Chapter 6

Dear Sue and Geoff,

Go on....open it...now that's what you call a muscle. I think up here they are called 'Clappidoos'. I only sent you a shell, I thought a live muscle would smell pretty bad after being in the post and you wouldn't be too pleased. They must be the 'Arnold Swartzanneger' of the muscle world.

Gwen and I have been picking wild raspberries, what a bore, they are by a road so I have to sit still, it takes ages to fill a container then I'm not even allowed to taste one. I heard her telling Paul the hazelnuts will be ripe soon, I'm putting my pad down and I am not going with her to pick them, she'll have me picking potatoes next.

We have been at Ardlamont for a couple of days. They have chickens everywhere but I'm not allowed to play with them, they are stupid looking creatures, Gwen likes them but that probably says it all. Paul's just given me a wink, he probably knows what I am thinking. Paul and I have been busy playing football, but he's not as fit as me so he's a bit stiff in his joints. Gwen says he's getting too old to play football and I should know better than to encourage him, so I'm in the dog house again.

Paul has dropped a hint of what he would like for Christmas. He has just bought a new digital camera so would now like a computer to be able to print off his photos. Gwen said if she bought a door would he build her a house to go round it. Paul said what he always says which is "yes dear".

If my two disagree on something it always end up with Paul saying "yes dear" and then he does what he wants anyway.

But I can tell you, he'll never cope with a digital camera, he struggles with those throw away jobbies.

I'm going for a wee snooze now, the winter sun is out and it's quite rare, it's just touching my kennel. Siesta time, unless they disturb me.

Take care,
HRH Traigh

We were looking forward to my nephew Nick and his wife Suzanne coming to stay, knowing that they would enjoy the area and also Traigh. Nick is my sister's son so they had read his previous letters and realised he would be a bit of a character.

Chapter 7

Dear Sue and Geoff,

I seem to have grown just a little taller, but the strange thing is Paul and Gwen haven't, so maybe they are not eating the right food. I did offer them some of mine, but they refused, so I can't do more than that now can I?

We also had visitors who you know very well, Nick and Suzanne, they took me to the shore at teatime to play (whilst Gwen was doing the cooking), Nick was very good at throwing my ball but Suzanne was rubbish, Gwen's not very good either, I expect it's a girlie thing.

Nick could not understand why I always returned to the same rock to drop the ball.

It's easy, Princess Diana had a rock so why can't I. (I am HRH after all.)

Gwen thinks I just lay in the lounge, but I watch all the documentaries, they are very educational, that's how I knew about the rock. I have to keep abreast of things, it all helps to educate them.

Talking of man things, which I suppose I wasn't, Bar-b-ques!!! How stupid are they, I am in favour of us chaps sticking together but I find this bit of masculinity so crazy. The men spend ages trying to light them, (apparently you can get gas ones, but Paul says they are cheating) then keep them lit whilst they have a beer, often they are all too busy talking by which time the charcoal needs topping up and then you have to wait again for it to get hot. WHY!

Just put it under the grill or in the oven and eat it outside (with all the flies for company).

Now Gwen often goes fishing at lunchtime if the tide is right and of course I go with her, as you know she's not really fit to be let out on her own, but why go to all that trouble when the 'fish man' comes on a Tuesdays in his van.

I sit and watch her for a while, but I get bored so I go and have a mooch about on the shore, forever keeping a quiet eye on her, just in case she falls off the edge of the pier.(Ok, I know I did it.)

It seems silly to throw a line into the water just to reel it back again and do it again and again and again. BORING.

Now when she catches something she says it's worth keeping, she bashes it on the head with a priest. Now, correct me if I am wrong but the documentaries I watch portray a priest as being a good man, not a murderer, so yes I am living with a murderer. It makes me feel uneasy, she has a side to her I have not seen before and all this so she can put up a sign that says 'Gone Fishing'.

I hope this is a nine-day wonder, but I don't think so, often we all go again after tea, now Paul's at it as well. There will be no fish left, I think you should tell The Minister of Agriculture and Fisheries about her, she's a danger to the planet. When she pops her clogs we should just push her over the end of the pier into the loch and then the fish can eat her and get their own back, cheaper too.

Gwen put flour in the fridge the other day, she thought I hadn't seen her, I tell you she is losing it, Paul said she lost it some time ago, the responsibility is getting too much for a dog of my tender years, I am getting old before my time.

My mate Duncan is leaving, he has bought his own park near Stranraer, I hope I spelt that right, I wouldn't want to insult him. I wish him well but I am going to miss him, when I need a break from my two I go over to stay with him. Wow! We have some fun, having a bud, chilling out, you know the sort of thing. He's getting married too. I have asked him if he is sure and he says he is, I just hope he knows what he is letting himself in for, after all I bet Gwen seemed normal at one time. Actually I know his future wife and she is lovely.

A lady who works and lives at Lochgoilhead has a cat called Smokey, it passes by to say hello now and then, but if it's raining it comes in my kennel and really there's just not enough room so I get out and sit on the roof. I'm just being a gentle soul, any canine should give up their seat for an elderly friend. Paul then has to give me a good towel down so I'm usually glad when Smokey calls by.

It's the Cowal Games today. They do something called Tossing the Caber. What rubbish, it's just chucking a piece of wood, then they throw the hammer, what on earth for, a hammer is for knocking nails in.

The men spend weeks talking about how they are going to THRASH each other, then get hold of a piece of rope and pull it backwards, TO GET AWAY FROM EACH OTHER.

After all this energetic stuff, there is a pipe band and fireworks but they won't take me to that, they think I might be scared, I'm no cissy, well maybe just a bit.

Anyway I must go Gwen's being awfully quiet, not a good sign, she'll be up to no good.

Bye for now,
HRH Traigh

Christmas was approaching and the Park was fairly quiet, we presume folk are busy Christmas shopping, although with not a lot of people about we're able to get things done that couldn't be done in the summer when we didn't want to disturb their bit of peace and quiet.

Chapter 8

Hello,

Okay, so it's nearly Christmas, who cares, I've only got one present so far, they keep telling me Santa has the rest, why has he got them and why do I have to wait until the 25th December? Why can't they just be here in the first place. You humans are really weird, give me Harry Potter any day, now he really is a wizard, his films are great.

Also it's the Christmas Olympia Horse Show, we watched it for four hours last night, Paul and I were getting really fed up, horses jump fences and they either do or they don't, and that's it, what's all the fuss about. It's more exciting watching paint dry.

They do show dog agility and that looks pretty good, Gwen says I am too big to do it, but I wouldn't mind giving it a go, it's Paul and Gwen that would be useless at it.

Thanks for my advent calendar, though it's a bit mean it only gives me one minute biscuit a day, mind you they didn't even buy me one. Gwen says "enjoy it whilst it lasts", come the 25th they are all gone. That's another stupid human saying, enjoy it whilst it lasts, once it's gone you can't enjoy it, it's finished.

Gwen and Paul are having Christmas dinner over in Inverary, I hope they remember they will be leaving me on my own for 3 hours AND on Christmas day!

I shall lounge about and watch TV and make them feel really guilty when they get back.

I am going to go and round up Paul now, can't have him winding down yet for Xmas, jobs to do, people to see and all that.

Have a good Christmas,
HRH Traigh

Christmas was pretty quiet on the Park, but much busier at New Year. Just after the New Year it started to rain heavily and continued its torrential downpour until it washed away the bridge at the end of the Park, once it had stopped, Crawford who works for the company came with a digger and scooped lots of stones and debris out of the burn. Hopefully if it happens again the water will flow away better.

Paul asked him to take a couple of extra scoops out at one particular place so that come the summer and it was hot Traigh had his own pool for cooling off.

Chapter 9

Dear Sue and Geoff,

Hope you had a lovely Christmas, I did. I got lots of presents, so the Santa bloke did come. My toy box is overflowing, it's now not a toy box, it's a brain stimulation box, I decided to change its name, my status is growing.

Gwen got a Steiff teddy bear, but she won't let me play with it, which I think is very unfair, I let her play with mine. It's got a button in its ear, seems rather silly, mine have them on their coats which is more logical, but we are talking about something that belongs to Gwen.

New Year was awful, we froze up and then had power cuts which went on for days. I was eating by candlelight, not too good, I like to see what I am eating to make sure it's up to my standard.

Gwen went to the doctors and she has got something called Meniere's disease which probably explains why she is so dizzy. I am being unkind, it is not very nice for her, she feels very dizzy and can fall over, she has tablets to take for a month, no alcohol and keep out of the sun. The sun wouldn't normally be a problem but they are going on holiday, some holiday she'll have, perhaps she should have a button in her ear.

It's the K9 god punishing her for leaving me in the kennels whilst they are away, we should have gone to Arisaig.

It's raining hard today and it's grey and miserable, but at least it's washing away the snow.

Take care,
HRH Traigh

Again summer seemed to pass by quickly and soon leaves were turning brown again, we were always busy yet still had a good routine for Traigh, at work things were always very varied so there was always plenty to talk about in the evenings.

Chapter 10

Hello.

So sorry not to have put pad to paper lately but I have been pretty busy.

The weather has been so very mixed, it's difficult to plan even a day in front let alone a week and as you know, old bossy boots likes to be organised.

I had a sleep over at a friend's and they were having a bar-b-que. I really needed the loo, but they were all so busy and not listening to me. I am not allowed to go on short cut grass, so I jumped the fence into the next-door neighbours and went there, well he should have cut his lawn, it was like a field. They were all roaring with laughter when they realised what I had done, I went red but they couldn't see because of my long coat.

Gwen has got a new hearing aid, the first one didn't work, so no wonder she wouldn't do a woof I said, she couldn't hear at all. She has also had an X-ray on her jaw and her problem is not arthritis, it could be muscular, so before they delve into her head, which is a complete waste of taxpayers' money, she has to take muscle-relaxing tablets, if she's any more laid back she'll be dead. Her problems are all in the same area, neck, ear and jaw, apparently the rest of her is fine, but even that is down to interpretation, they don't live with her.

Another 6 weeks and then we are on 2 days off a week, can't wait, maybe we'll do things I want to do, although last week we went to the beach at Ardentinny and they did the silly barby thing. It was very good though, it was really warm and Paul and I swam for ages. Gwen didn't, she read a book, if she didn't have a book to read I swear she would *read the labels on a bean tin, she has to have a book in her hand. Trouble is she has no taste, she reads murder mysteries and biographies, I have told her to get a proper education and read things like Lassie Come Home but I just get 'The Look'.*

There are Army manoeuvres going on around Lochgoilhead again. One moment you are driving down the glen and then a chap in combat gear and a dirty face comes out of the scrub and gives you the fright of your life. I cannot believe they are allowed out without having a wash.

Last week they must have been new recruits because they were so young, Paul saw two of them struggling with large rucksacks and asked if they were okay. They had to get to the rendezvous by a certain time and they were not going to make it. Paul put them in the back of his van and gave them a lift close to where they should be, poor kids they were soaking. It was only a little cheat, well about 3 miles of a cheat.

Today we have had a helicopter landing in the boatyard, collecting sand and taking it further down the Loch. Why not just use a lorry? The noise is driving me mad, so much for the peace and quiet of the glen.

Gwen and I went out at lunchtime and we saw a Naval Vessell coming into Loch Goil and honestly we hadn't taken our eyes off it for long and we saw it was going the other way, out of the Loch. Gwen said it must have done a handbrake turn, even I know they don't have a handbrake.

As you know the old girl is 50 next, the present you posted up is the only one in the wardrobe, I bet it's all she gets. Actually I shall get her a present, some hair dye, oh boy is she going grey. If she uses a coppery coloured dye, her head looks like a lump of rusty steel, I try not to look or she'll hear me having a crafty whine, I don't know how Paul keeps his face straight, practise I suppose. Mind you, he can't laugh really, he is losing his hair fast. Will I go bald when I get old, some of my pals have gone a bit grey around the face?

Take care,
HRH Traigh

My 50th had crept up on me and I didn't like to think I was on my way to 60, but then I thought, just get on with it, it's only a number, so common sense stepped in and I decided to enjoy life and I did.

Chapter 11

Hi,

I hear you are coming up for a holiday, Gwen says I have to find a large flashing light to keep you awake at night because that's how you remember caravan holidays, she said the Lighthouse at Flamborough was to blame.

The midges really bite so you'll have to use some repellent, there's lots of it here, although Gwen still hasn't found one that works for her.

I am going to take you fishing off the little pier, we shall catch mackerel and as soon as we get back we can smoke them, they will be really fresh and I know you love fish, Gwen told me.

It's funny to think I shall be able to look at you, as I have never seen you before I wonder if you will look like you do in my imagination. Gwen says you don't look like her, what a bonus for you.

Paul and Gwen have just comeback from the Highland Show, I had to go to the kennels, they said I wouldn't like being surrounded by thousands of legs and not being able to see anything, but it would have been nice to make my own mind up.

Gwen and I were coming over the Glen yesterday which is a single-track road and there is one place that is a long stretch of road with a passing place. A small car was coming in the opposite direction and we expected the driver to pull in, so we slowed down politely and then when we passed Gwen would put her hand up to say the usual thank you. But no, the lady in the car stopped and waved at Gwen to reverse back, now normally Gwen would just do so, but as this lady was only one car length from the pull in she decided not to.

The lady was furious and was waving her hands about and shouting. Gwen turned off our engine and went to ask what was wrong. The lady said Gwen had to reverse as there was no way she was pulling into the space, her car would get DIRTY and to hurry up, she was in a rush.

I heard Gwen say very quietly "you're going to have a long wait then", she slowly walked back to the car and picked up a Horse and Hound magazine. This woman, I'm not going to call her a lady anymore started blowing her horn and screaming. Gwen ignored her completely and it's one time that Gwen being a bit deaf was a bonus. Eventually she did pull into the passing place and Gwen started the car and drove past to much verbal abuse but Gwen just gave her 'the look'.

Right time for a quick bite to eat and I must get on. I enclose Paul and Gwen's new mobile numbers, but sorry I'm ex-directory.

Bye,
HRH Traigh

We had decided that Traigh could have a treat box, so we used a biscuit tin and in the evening he was allowed two little treats but he never had them at any other time. We would take the lid off the box and he could choose. If he picked out three by mistake he would just pick one up and put it back. This was around 8.00pm and if we forgot, he would go to the cupboard and wait patiently for us to get up and get his tin. He had pieces of dental sticks and very small biscuits in it.

Chapter 12

Dear Sue and Geoff,

I hear you have been on holiday, I hope you had a great time.

On the 21ˢᵗ October we had the first snow of the year, it's cold, but looks very nice. We went walking up Glen Coe Mountains and you could look down with cloud below you, it was brilliant, it was like looking down on cotton wool. I think I could be a weather reporter, I would make the weather imaginative.

Gwen and Paul have changed doctors, they had to go for a new patient check-up. Gwen was insulted because he said they drank too much, they share a bottle of wine over dinner but he said it was too much. I believe Paul said "Cobblers" or words to that effect.

He then asked Gwen if she wanted HRT, now I am confused I thought I was the HR. Paul laughed all the way home, but I don't know what about, perhaps you could enlighten me, they certainly won't.

My two went to Norfolk and I went to the kennels. It's time I went away for a holiday so I am thinking about going on a singles holiday. I got a Saga brochure, but it's not for me, I want to party. I better look again.

Paul fancies a camper van, but Gwen says he just wants to be an aging hippie, with his fishing hat and shades he looks more like one of the Blues Brothers (if you have a good imagination).

Take care,
HRH Traigh

My sister Sue was not at all well and we were concerned for her. Also around this time we were approached by a company who asked us to go and look at a Park in Northumberland with the view to being general managers. We thought long and hard and in the end decided if we didn't go and look we would be foolish. It was a large park with static holiday home, tents, tourers and also motorhome pitches. It had a lake, a clubhouse with lots of entertainment and food served and also a children's indoor and outdoor play area and swimming pool. It was not far from the coast and the Park owners seemed extremely nice. We came home and decided we would move.

It wasn't an easy decision, we knew leaving Argyll would be difficult and it was. On our last day we were asked to stay and a tempting offer was made, but we had given our word and it could not be broken.

Chapter 13

Hello you two,

Sorry to hear that you are unwell and in hospital Sue, it's the best place for you, well that's what everyone says but I expect the truth is that it is exceedingly boring.

I am slowly getting used to living in Northumberland, (where is Southumberland?) the beaches are great, especially the one at Bamborough, that's my favourite. The park has a massive dog walking field, it has plenty of rabbits and pheasants and it is funny watching other dogs trying to chase them. We also walk up into the Cheviot Hills a lot and they are beautiful, nowhere near as dramatic as Scotland but still very pleasant.

My two are going to head office down in the Lakes tomorrow and I am staying with Jed, he works on the park, he's nice, he has a Spaniel which is lovely, but quite stupid. It doesn't get enough exercise so it's silly, I have been told in no uncertain terms not to get any ideas. Spoil sports.

The park opens the second week in March and Gwen is going demented trying to interview seasonal staff. Some of the interviewees should be residing in an asylum certainly not wanting a job facing the general public. One vacancy is for a receptionist, she doesn't need someone with a degree in sociology, just plain common sense and politeness. Common sense is not easily available, she should give me the job, I could do it all except make the tea.

Paul is sick of building wardrobes, he didn't realise just how many Gwen had ordered. The table legs arrived today, fancy sending a dining set without legs. They can now eat properly at the table, although they have been managing in a fashion.

Paul propped up the table on four of the chairs and some boxes so they were able to eat at each end of the table, but there was no room to put their legs under so they sat sideways and got indigestion, at least the lounge is done, it looks lovely.

Must get Paul to post this straight away then it will get the Saturday lunchtime post, his secretarial duties are coming on a treat, but I don't give him one of those, if I can't have one during the day, then neither can he.

Get well soon,
HRH Traigh

Seasonal staff were eventually found and after a gloomy start weather wise and after the usual winter frost problems we were open for business.

Chapter 14

Hi,

Are you feeling any better??

The Park opened at the weekend and lots of people had burst pipes, especially on the lake field, you could hardly tell where the lake stopped and the caravans started. The owners kept saying things like "we haven't had frost at home". Right, you live in the Caribbean then. Paul said he wished he had a pound for every lie that came through the door.

I am having a great laugh at Gwen's expense, where we are, all the women are called 'hen'. Gwen hates it. Can you imagine her re-incarnated as a hen? I can, it would be perfect, 'cluck cluck here, boss boss there, here there and everywhere'. Perfect description of Gwen. Gwen with feathers!!! The mind boggles.

We have one or two (ten or twenty) owners that let their dogs foul on the Park, Paul's pet hate, anyway he caught one of them, so he asked him to get a bag and remove it. After the man called Paul a few choice words, he was told he had 15 minutes to walk back to his touring caravan and get a bag or his caravan would be on the road in thirty minutes.

Amazing, word got round and there have been no more 'incidents' of people forgetting to carry bags and all other complaints are being made most politely.

I have found polite complaints are usually genuine, it's the shouters that are usually upset about something else and just want to let off steam.

They are shown the door and asked to come back when they have cooled down.

We are having a fish delivery this week, now I got a bit muddled because I thought they came in a white van and were filleted and ready for the grill. These are alive and will go into the trout lake, but what's the point, Gwen will then go and catch them and fillet them for supper, so we might as well have had the white van in the first place.

We don't eat just as much fish as what we did in Scotland. Gwen is really struggling to be away from Argyll, to be truthful. Paul and I are the same but we are trying to be brave and not show it. The walks here are good, but not as good as climbing so high the RAF jets are below you. I miss that.

Hope the doctors sort you out soon, if they do then tell them to start on Gwen, that'll keep them busy.

Bye.
HRH Traigh

Traigh is right about the complainers, we had one lady complain bitterly there were not enough trees for shade and it was too hot, she didn't like it when it was too warm. So why go camping in the outdoors? Just stay at home with all the doors and windows closed, keep the curtains shut and be a misery all on your own.

Chapter 15

Dear Sue and Geoff,

It's just a short note to tell you about my visit to the vet on Tuesday.

The waiting room is in the reception area and there was a very pretty black Labrador waiting patiently, so I decided to sit next to her and say hello, actually I said "Good afternoon". I wanted to impress, she replied in a very refined way. She's a bit older than me but it doesn't matter these days does it.

The vet asked her owner to "bring her in" and Gwen looked at me and said "Stay". Why I have no idea, I would not move unless she said so and she knows that. Well the man got up and went into the treatment room but the Labrador had listened to Gwen and didn't move, he had to come back for her, he was embarrassed and so was I, so I don't suppose I'll see her again.

When it was my turn, he called me Tray, I corrected him and he apologised so all was well. He looked at my teeth and said they had a bit of tartar on them, I thought that was what you humans called a stuffy person. My ears are fine thank goodness, can't have two of us with dodgy ears.

Then he went right down in my estimation, he said I was fat, actually I have put on a pound or two since the beginning of January, Gwen wanted to know how much, he said I should be about 23 kilo's and I was 25, so I think saying I was fat was just insulting. Since the move I haven't been doing just as much in the evenings but Paul and I are back into our routine again so it will roll off me. Both Paul and I will be ship shape soon.

When he asked me to sit on his scales I just obliged and went over to them, but he forgot to tell me to get off them, he looked round surprised to see me still there and said "so sorry old chap, forgot you were there". It was really funny.

I then had to have my annual flu and distemper jab and also my kennel cough, he turned his back on me whilst he got ready and I told him he needn't hide the needle from me, I was no baby. He asked Gwen to hold me but she said no, I would be offended just ask him to sit still and he will, which of course I did, he then put the squirty liquid up my nose for the kennel cough, it always makes me want to sneeze, but as I didn't have a tissue I just had to wiggle the end of my nose until I felt better.

He said I was an absolutely model patient and his job would be so easy if all the dogs were like me, I grew a couple of inches. I then laid down (and crossed my paws) as Gwen and him talked about different methods of dog training and he asked if she would be interested in doing training. Gwen thought he meant for us to go, but he actually meant for Gwen to take the classes as the current trainers dog was nowhere near as good as me. Gwen said thank you but no, she had enough to do, he asked her to ring him if she changed her mind.

On the way home I told Gwen that I would object, I don't want her training every Tom, Dick and Lassie.

The next day we went back to Lochgoilhead so Gwen and Paul could go to the dentist. We were driving up Loch Lomond and Gwen started to cry, neither Paul or I realised just how homesick she was, she just couldn't stop, it was awful. I think the scenery just got to her, I could see Paul was blinking a lot, he said he had something in his eye, but it could have been because he felt so sorry for her.

In the end we had a lovely day and saw lots of folk we knew, but it was hard to drive out of the glen again.

Take care,
HRH Traigh

Being at Wooler we were only 17 miles away from the Scottish border and days off usually meant we crossed it.

Every week we said we would go somewhere different but the car seemed determined to cross into Scotland. We were enjoying the work but I particularly pined to be north of the border.

Chapter 16

Dear Sue and Geoff,

We all walked to the village today and it seems that everyone is related to each other. There are some very nice people in Wooler, everyone wanted to stop and have a chat and say hello to me.

A member of the Berwick Swan and Wildlife Trust came to see Gwen last week to discuss putting a couple of Swans on the lake. One of them has only one wing so will never fly, the other one is okay, just weak so may eventually fly away, anyway we released them on Monday and they seem to have settled in fine. Three young Mallards were also released but we could not see them this morning when we walked the lake, perhaps they were in the undergrowth on the island.

Paul and Gwen consulted me and we decided it would be a good idea to put a CCTV camera facing down the drive towards the road, it would be fastened to the end of the office. A tree was in the way so Gwen asked one of the ground staff to take it down to leave just one metre in the ground as it would be perfect to put notices on, everyone would see them driving into the park.

The road was cordoned off at both ends, hard hat, protective gear and high visibility jackets were donned and our chain saw operator fired up the chain saw. Gwen went to answer the phone, came back to find the hard hat and high-viz jacket on the floor and the tree taken right down to ground level.

To say she was not pleased is an understatement, he said he was too hot, couldn't see with the hat on and had forgotten about leaving a metre in the ground.

So all that was left was a trip hazard and I saw Gwen give him that 'look'.

This same chap also had the habit of leaving the tractor running unattended whilst he went into the shop or went to talk to somebody. Paul told him this could not happen as children could get into it. So whilst he turned off the engine he never remembered to take the keys out so one day Gwen jumped in and hid the tractor. Back in the office Gwen watched out of the window to see him scratching his head and looking worried, pacing the ground where the tractor had been.

Eventually he came in and said the tractor must have been stolen and Gwen said how on earth could anyone steal a locked tractor. He was very apologetic and admitted he had left the keys in it. Gwen took the keys out of her office drawer and told him where it was, it was the last time he did it.

Take care, will be in touch again soon,
HRH Traigh

Wooler is a nice village with one of the best cheese shops I have ever encountered, locally produced cheeses that just asked to be eaten. It had a variety of shops which seemed to cater for everyone. If we wanted a larger supermarket we would drive to Berwick-upon-Tweed but we tried to shop locally as much as possible.

Chapter 17

Hello,

It's so windy here, people are trying to hold on to tents and awnings. Tempers are fraying along with the canvasses, kids are crying because they cannot stay on their bikes for the wind, rubbish is flying in all directions and then we had a power cut. A typical bank holiday. The whole area went out, but of course some people thought it was our fault, as if we did it on purpose just so they could have a moan. Roll on next week and we can get back to proper campers who walk and fish, ramble and enjoy and respect the countryside, not these city numpties.

One townie complained about a funny smell. Yes manure, we live in the countryside. He wanted a refund because it wasn't mentioned in the brochure. Gwen said he was welcome to go and ask the farmer, he was pretty annoyed as he said he doesn't get it back home to which Gwen replied, "No dairy farming hasn't hit the centre of Newcastle yet." Thikko, he didn't even realise she was being sarky and boy can she be sarky when she wants to.

The swans seem to be okay, the wind might upset them a little but I'm sure they will be fine.

On Thursday we went walking in the hills above Wooler, it's just a bit like the Dales, lovely stone walls and lots of sheep which all watched me quite suspiciously as I walked past them, I felt as if I was on a cat walk. Why is it called a catwalk?

To be honest I did look good, I have purchased a new brush and it is very good and also Gwen had clipped my claws. I just don't walk on enough hard ground so every so often Gwen gives them a little clip, I don't mind she makes a good job of it, far better than going to one of them 'Parlours', have you seen the sights that come out of them? Ponsy dogs with ribbons in their hair and even painted toenails. It's ridiculous and giving us proper dogs a bad name. If you can't have a pint and go rabbiting with the lads it's a poor do.

Some of them even have Barbour jackets and pretend they are the country set and they fold their jackets inside out so you can see the label yet they never get their pads dirty. It's the parents I blame, they weren't born to be so stupid surely, I don't know what the world's coming to.

Well I'm going back to work now, I'm off to walk the lake and check the fishing permits, Paul has promoted me to 'Chief water bailiff', hope you are impressed.

Bye for now,
HRH Traigh.

The Park was still busy and Paul and I think if you manage a Park then you should walk it every day. People will come out to talk to you, whereas they probably won't come into the office, this is especially true of older folk, they don't like to bother you. This meant with a large park Traigh got lots of walks and lots of attention which of course he loved.

Traigh and I would sometimes walk to the bank but we were stopped such a lot that I felt guilty as I should be at work, so we went back to driving up to the village to pay in at the bank which obviously didn't take so long.

Chapter 18

Hello, how are you?

Just needed to tell you about Caroline. Caroline works in the office and on Saturday she came into the bar and wanted to ask for a packet of pickled onion crisps but instead she asked for crippled onion picks, it was pretty funny.

We have been really busy and working silly hours but we are fully staffed again so things should settle down a bit, I have to say my two are absolutely ......, I'd better say tired, I'm not allowed to use naughty words.

On Saturday they had a lovely letter from Phill and Carol saying how pleased they were and gave us a salary rise to show their appreciation, wasn't that nice. I might get a new squashy toy now, Rudolph has only one ear and one leg. I keep showing it to everyone who knocks on the door in the hope it will shame them into the toyshop. As yet it hasn't worked.

One of the swans tried to fly on Friday and crash-landed at the far end of the Park.

Gwen took a couple of men with her to catch it but they were none too keen on the idea as they can be aggressive, anyway Gwen caught it and got one of the chaps to drive her back to the lake. There were an awful lot of stares as Gwen had it on her knee in the front of the truck with its head out of the window. I told her there was no way it was going in the back with me, it might bite. Gwen said I was a wimp.

Paul said it had slavered down the back of the passenger seat (a miracle when it had its head out of the window) anyway I saw Gwen going out with a cloth just in case.

The swans are a novelty at the moment and are getting fed a lot. The people know to soak the bread first so it doesn't swell up inside their stomachs, but of course the fish are eating it too and therefore not taking the fishermen's flies. It's very hard to please everyone in fact its damned impossible. Is 'damned' swearing??

At least I'm easily pleased.

Be good,
HRH Traigh

The swan incident was talked about for a long time and I expect it was funny to see. Swans can live a long time and we hope they would be around for years to come, they added a grace to the waters.

Chapter 19

Hi,

Very short letter, in fact it's only a note.

Today is the Northumbrian Fell Race where loonies run 22 miles over hill and dale or I suppose fell and valley. The day started with the alarm going off at 5.00 AM, needless to say I turned over and ignored it.

I decided eventually to go and have a look and support the ones running for charity. The place is swarming with blokes thinking they are God's gift in shorts, some of them should be banned unless they cover up. UGH! It should be the eleventh commandment, arrogant men can't wear shorts, then there should be a twelfth, fat women can't wear leggings.

I imagine I've just upset a few folk, never mind I am allowed my opinion. Freedom of speech and all that, power to the canines.

Also my two have bought me new transport at last, it's a 4x4 crew cab and the back bit (which is mine) is really big so I can party if I want, but not to Gwen's music, it's rubbish. Paul thinks I am spoilt and says it's an expensive dog kennel, Gwen even had tinted windows fitted for me to shade me from the sun, but I'm worth it.

Bye,
HRH Traigh

We had been at Wooler for only six months although it felt a lot longer. The park owner had come up to see us and asked if we would go look at a Park near Ashbourne in Derbyshire as he would like us to move and manage it.

We set off not knowing what to expect, the park was by the Tissington Trail (a great walking and cycling path) just north of Ashbourne. No clubhouse but a nice small pool, excellent children's play area and 78 acres of mixed land.

We came home and decided being farther away from Scotland might be beneficial as hopefully we wouldn't be so homesick knowing we couldn't just nip back over the border and we would see the children more. Guy and Louise were both in their mid-20s and busy doing their own thing and both seemed pretty happy but it would be nice to be a bit nearer.

So we moved.

Chapter 20

Dear Sue and Geoff,

I quite like living here, the garden is lovely and the Park is 78 acres so lots of walking for me. Some of it is down to woodland so again great for me.

Nick and Suzanne came down and said the Park looked lovely, pair of fibbers, there was mud everywhere and the park looked a real mess, can't compete with mother nature, when she wants it to rain, it rains.

The cooker arrived, but the gasman didn't, well he did eventually so all is well. Paul and Gwen are fighting over whose doing the cooking, won't affect me as they don't cook mine.

Guess what? They are now officially certified. They had to take courses on how to use a grass cutter, tractor, manual handling. Gwen took her personal licence for the sale of alcohol and Paul took his pool plant operators license and they both did first aid.

I went to a couple of them with them to be sure they were alright. The chap who did manual handling was a right clever clogs, I kept my eye on him. His introduction was to ask if anyone could guarantee they would not put their back out lifting anything and Gwen said "Yes she could" when questioned about her confidence in this she replied, "That's why these chaps are employed, I ask them to do it." He sort of humphed (like a horse), real cocky sort.

The guy taking the tractor course thought Gwen was there to make the tea, wrong, I did try to warn him but he ignored me. He was quite nice though, very polite, but I bet he felt a prat.

A couple on the Park have a little young King Charles Spaniel, apparently the kids wanted a dog so they bought this young pup and they got fed up of him. Typical of some humans, just don't look further than the end of their noses. They wanted to rid of him, Gwen rang Paul's sister Karen, as they had lost their King Charles not long ago, difficult because you don't know if you are doing the right thing or not.

Karen, Peter and the three kids came down on Friday and now he has a new home and will be looked after really well. He is called Charlie and I am happy to say he is a very different character to Benjy who they lost, so they won't be able to compare and it will make it easier for them. Benjy was very laid back whereas Charlie just wants to play constantly, but all is well that ends well, one big happy family.

I'm busy out on the Park today with Paul, we are painting, well, I am supervising. Gwen is stuck in the office and it's a nice day, for once I feel sorry for her, but don't let on.

Bye for now.
HRH Traigh

I got stuck into the garden and made a vegetable plot in the back and Paul made some planters for the front. It had a lovely Derbyshire stone wall round it and soon it looked established and the vegetables grew brilliantly in the fertile Derbyshire soil. Green beans were abundant and we were giving them away to everyone, I have never worked on such good soil.

There was a weasel living in the wall that was around the top end of the front garden and Traigh would not go anywhere it, we wondered if he had got a nip from it as he gave that area a very wide berth.

Chapter 21

Hello,

Living here is okay, the house is nice and the garden is great, BUT I do not like all the banging noises. Gwen says its shooting season and lots of folk go out with guns and shoot birds. I don't want to go out in case someone misses and hits me.

I know Gwen thinks I am being silly, but I just don't like it, at least Paul understands.

I like the bottom of the Park the best, its woodland and a stream runs through it, it's not used by the holidaymakers, so I think it's just mine. Sometimes Gwen or Paul brings me down at lunchtime, they have a sandwich sat on a log and I have a paddle and go into the undergrowth. Paul says it's like a jungle but I don't know what a jungle is.

The only down side is there is no sea and I miss my swimming. I have asked if I can go in the pool but they both said no. I did expect Gwen to say no, so I went behind her back and asked Paul, I can't believe he said no too, he's usually the easy one; I can normally get anything from him.

The Park closes down at the end of October and opens again at Easter. I thought we would be quiet but we have a great winter programme to do and I am going to have brilliant fun.

Gwen says you are coming down for the day and compared to Scotland it will be a very short drive.

Look forward to seeing you soon,
HRH Traigh.

As October approached the seasonal staff left for the winter and the quite silly hours we had put in over the summer were calculated to even out how many hours we would do in the winter. I think it was about 12 hours a week. We had two members of staff stay over winter, so allowing for holidays away there was still always someone on the Park.

Chapter 22

Hi, how are you?

Wow! It's really quiet as everyone has left for the winter. I like it, I don't have to be on a lead at all and I have acres and acres to play in, but I don't go far away from them, I like to see what they are up to.

Today Paul and I have been in the top field that has Static caravans in and I keep 'finding' balls that children have left. I keep taking them back to my garden, then go looking for another one, I have had a good day today, I have found five. Paul says I will be in trouble when Easter comes, but it seems so far away I'm not going to think about it, anyway they should have put them away and not leave them lying about.

If I didn't put my things away in the evening I would be in big trouble.

The indoor swimming pool is being partially filled in so it's not so deep and then I heard Paul telling Gwen that there is going to be a new plant fitted. I found this conversation very difficult to keep up to, because to me a plant is something that grows, (or doesn't when it comes to Gwen keeping plants inside). Bless her she can grow anything outdoors, but inside no. Paul bought her one of those air plants that don't really need looking after, it died!

It appears this 'plant' is to automatically look after the swimming pool and put in the correct chemicals and it takes readings all the time. Once again I am confused I thought you read a book.

Oh well, just keep turning the pages, I've still got lots to tell you.

Take care,
HRH Traigh

The new instalment for the pool took up space in the garage, but it was so much better than before when you had to go underneath the pool to look at the dials. Both Paul and I kept banging our heads on the beams that presumably held up the pool floor, if we had been any taller we would have had to practically crawl to the pipes and meters.

Traigh couldn't understand why we would ask him to wait outside, but there were rusty nails on the floor and although we kept picking them up we would always find more the next day. We would come out to find him laid down with his head on crossed paws.

Chapter 23

Dear Sue and Geoff,

The winter has passed much gentler than it did in Scotland, but I miss it.

The park has opened again and it's busy with folk opening up their holiday homes to let the fresh air in after the winter.

We were eagerly (sorry it's a lie, no we were not) waiting for the first to complain and Paul got him.

This man was complaining about moles, as there were molehills around and under his static caravan in an area that was nicknamed 'Crinkly Bottom' due to the age of most of its occupants.

Paul said he already knew and the man wanted to know how. Paul said the mole had been in earlier complaining that some idiot had dropped a big green tin thing on top of his house. Unfortunately the man didn't have a sense of humour. I was nearly whining with laughter.

Last week was Spring Bank and it poured down, absolutely typical bank holiday weather. Gwen had taken a booking for a tent with one adult and two children. A lady arrived in white high-heeled shoes with two little boys about 8 years old dressed as if they were going to a wedding. Apparently she wanted to give them 'the camping experience' whatever that is.

She was shown where to pitch her tent, but she was back in two minutes. "Oh I can't possibly stay there, it's muddy." We are in the countryside, it has rained for days and it's a flat field. Poor soul, her shoes were dirty, I felt sorry for the two boys I bet they would have loved to get dirty. Gwen just handed her money back and suggested she booked into a hotel in Ashbourne. I won't tell you what Gwen called her.

Within twenty minutes the pitch had been re-booked by a man with his 12 years old son. They were hiking in waterproofs and big smiles on their faces, pity the snooty woman hadn't seen how happy they were, perhaps then her boys could have had some fun. I bet they really miss out on life, what a shame.

Right must go, I'm on pass checking duty. AGAIN.

Be good,
HRH Traigh

There was always something happening and the days passed quickly, Guy came to see us, as did Louise and Andy and it was good to see them. Louise and Andy had a little girl, our first grandchild called Sophie which was lovely. Traigh wasn't sure about this thing that sometimes cried and when she did he went into the office out of the way but in years to come they played together often. So the time was pleasant but always there was something missing. We knew what it was, we just didn't want to admit it.

In the September Paul and I went to the caravan show which previews the new models for the coming season and met our old boss Keith from Lochgoilhead, a conversation ensued and it was obviously mutual that we wanted to go back and he wanted us to.

We went back to Derbyshire and then away on holiday in the December. Whilst away we had a phone call from him and on our return we headed north back 'home' to see the Park they had asked us to manage.

We handed in our notice at Derbyshire and received a nice letter of thanks and good wishes from the owners and we are still in touch now.

At the end of January we had moved back and took over the running of Stratheck Holiday Park by Loch Eck.

Chapter 24

Dear Sue and Geoff,

The weather has welcomed us back to Scotland, its pouring down and we have terrific wind. That's the weather not Paul and Gwen.

The Park is great and just across the road there are brilliant walks that radiate in all directions, it's just fantastic. Folks have welcomed us back with open arms, it's been just lovely.

The bungalow is being ripped apart as I dictate and work being done in lots of areas. It's a nice place although the garden is going to take forever, it's like a building site, but hey-ho, it's lovely to be home.

I asked Paul for a new kennel and I have to put in the design by Wednesday. Keith at Lochgoilhead asked his joiners to build his dog a new kennel, which they did, complete with balcony, chimney and a sign saying 'No entry, staff only'. Brilliant.

Take care.
HRH Traigh

We stayed in a caravan whilst the bungalow was being done, I could almost guarantee that if I needed something it was in a box 'somewhere' and not in the caravan. With it being early in the year there was not too many people on the Park and it gave us the opportunity of taking stock of what wanted doing. Paul is very particular as to how the ground looks and always puts his stamp on things. I enjoy the planting side of it and was looking forward to bedding plants arriving in the spring and also what was going to appear, that for the moment was hidden underground.

Chapter 25

Hi,

The sky is blue, it's very cold and there is snow on the hills, it looks just as I remember but come Thursday, our day off, it will pour down.

Gwen chopped the end of her finger off last night cutting up some bacon. No need to panic, she didn't chop the lot off, just the end but it wouldn't stop bleeding and the blood was sort of pulsing out. There was no point in going to the hospital because there was nothing to stitch and anyway the end of her finger was lost in the bacon.

She sat with her arm above her head for about an hour. It did eventually slow down and stop but it must have been sore because she was very quiet and that's not like Gwen at all.

Paul said he was glad we are going to be living in a bungalow with Gwen not having much upstairs. I expect he means brains, but I'm not sure.

The bungalow is coming along fine, I'm sure the chaps are doing more than they should, they have been really excellent. Robert the painter gets confused, he comes in to find a door where there was not one the day before, or ones been blocked up, he says he needs a map.

The carpet man is due today so it shouldn't be long before we can get settled.

My friend Mollie died on Sunday, she was only 10. Mollie owned Davy and Iona, Davy is devastated, it's not long since he lost his father. Mollie used to stay with Davy's mum and dad through the day and Davy's dad walked with Mollie a lot. Mollie carried on going as Davy's mum felt better with Mollie in the house.

Davy buried Mollie at the bottom of the garden, maybe she's now back with Davy's dad, I hope so, people believe that, don't they.

Gwen's been at the dental hospital and she has to wear a splint through the day, so she'll be stuttering, stammering and spitting all over the customers, fine way to sell a holiday home. I had better look in my diary and see if I have time to help her, I have, but if I get a better offer, I'm off, she doesn't pay enough and I do have commitments.

We have two new Highland cattle in the front field, one is black and one is a rusty colour. Paul has called them Jet and Duracell (copper coloured top) they are not very friendly, I tried to be nice but they are just ignorant, in fact rather snobbish. I'll have the last laugh because it's they who will be in the freezer and not me.

Bye for now,
HRH Traigh

We were very busy but enjoying it all enormously. There is always lots to do and it's great watching our hard work, especially the planting come to fruition.

Chapter 26

I have decided to join Gwen and go onto sales full time, I need the save for my retirement.

I put together the following letter that I am going to send out to all the owners but I need some feedback, what do you think...

Dear owner,

I would like to Traigh (see what I did there) to take the opportunity of introducing myself to you...

My name is Traigh and I am the purveyor of fancy goods and seller of holiday homes, large or small, old or new, wood or aluminium, with or without leaks.

I am the one with a full head of hair (moulting), 20/20 vision (spot a punter from a mile away) figure of a canine film star. I am approachable (open to bribery), keen to sort out your problems (pass the buck) and always available, (Mondays 10-1 weather permitting).

After being head hunted from the jungles of outer Forfar, (further north) I find myself with a selection of good second hand holiday homes for sale. I also have a number of new shiny ones not yet out of the wrappers.

Here's the deal, you give me your old one and we negotiate a sum of money as well. I can also do finance (APR 2756%) STS and depending on how I feel. Please ring the lukewarm sales line for more details.

OBVIOUSLY A JOKE, BUT THE NEXT BIT'S NOT.

Now below is a little quiz, it spells out something that will help me upgrade my Ferrari. First correct answer will genuinely win a bottle of wine and you can even choose red or white. Please send you completed entry to The Caravan and Chalet office marked for my attention. Good Luck.

Yours as sincerely as a sales person can be........Traigh,

What do you see out of, singular?
What material comes from trees?
What rhymes with bike and means I want that?
What number comes after one?
What three-letter word means cheerio?
What is the first letter of the alphabet?
What do you need after working non-stop, a?
Complete the phrase, "There's no place like?"

Name.........................Plot number..................

Spring arrived and soon we were busy meeting all the owners and their children, their dogs, cats and even the occasional budgie. Bicycles were peddled furiously and games of hide and seek were played and water pistol fights were the order of the day. The children (and us) had a great time. It was lovely to see children play out and amuse themselves without the need of a computer.

They all got on really well and there was very little 'falling out'. Happy and amused children meant that the adults could relax and Stratheck had exactly that atmosphere.

Chapter 27

Hello again,

My peace will be shattered tonight, they are having a karaoke night in the bar and the police will be on the Park later because I heard a chap say he's going to murder some songs. That's not very nice is it? Although if Gwen sings the place will shut early, everyone will leave, Paul says she can't hold a note but that's not true I've seen her holding her shopping list.

Paul has been busy in the old kitchen, he has partitioned it so that we will have a little study and a boot room, be good to make them take off their dirty boots at the door, because of the boot room the study is L shaped and it's lovely. Paul says we have to get a steamer as the wallpaper must be stuck on with superglue. He could save his money and just use Gwen, she's full of hot air.

Monday evening took us over the water to buy a new telly, it was a compromise that ended up in it being a 37 inch and I agree with Gwen for once, it looks just fine. Whilst we were there we also bought a blender/juicer thing. They must need their food mushing up so I expect it will soon be time for the dentist and false teeth.

Gwen put some fruit in it and switched it on, loads of black smoke came out of it, she was furious, the kitchen stunk. So whilst Paul was playing with his new telly, Gwen was cursing in the kitchen.

On Wednesday, Gwen bought 'things' to tie her hair up and then had it cut on Thursday. She's the talk of Stratheck, it's very short at the back and a bit (and I mean a bit) like Victoria Beckham at the front. She has also had some streaks put in but they are very subtle, not at all in character.

We are all very excited as it's not raining.

Our friend James who is in the Army has just had his passing out parade at Purbright. He is going into the Paratroop regiment and although they have to learn to parachute they are not allowed to jump into enemy territory for health and safety reasons. Perhaps he's just winding Paul up, but I might just google it. He has also just passed his marksman's course, Paul said as he can't hit a pool ball, he doubts if he can hit a barn door with a rifle so the enemy should be safe.

Take care,
HRH Traigh

The bar opened and we would sometimes go and have a game of pool and a chat with the owners. There were some good pool players and although competitive it was always played in good spirit.

There was always plenty of leg pulling at the bar between rival football supporters, but again usually in fun, it was rare for us to have to say "hey, enough now" and if we did it ended with them having a handshake and buying each other a pint.

Chapter 28

Dear Sue and Geoff,

My two are at it again, they took me to see the QE2, now why should I want to go and stand in the freezing cold and watch a ship sail out of the Clyde? You know that advert on TV, comfused.com, well that's me.

Now it was lovely and was built here so I can understand the humans wanting to see it but really they could have left me at home, I was busy studying nature (I was wondering why the trees go brown).

My pal said that Ark Royal was out to sea waiting for the QE2, he said it was a big boat for posh pets, that's why it's called Ark! I think he's making it up, he is a bit whacky, anyway if it is I'd be okay, what with being Royal and all that so I felt a bit smug.

There were loads of people as well as my two watching, they were toasting her with champagne and cheering, I have no idea why, the ship wouldn't hear them, it has no ears. This ship was blasting its horn really loud and Paul and Gwen thought this was great, why? They hate folk that blast their horn for no reason. Now all this silly business must be catching because even I have been calling this ship a her. It's a big lump of metal that floats, how can it be a her? I think I need to get two more pets, my two are making me as daft as them.

The other day Paul got up and gave me my breakfast and went out, then Gwen got up and made my breakfast too, I didn't want to seem ungrateful so I ate it, then she wanted to go out for a walk, but I didn't want to go, I was just too full.

Can you have a word with Paul, he might listen to you, I have been asking for over a week for carpet for my kennel to no avail, yet last night they were talking about beds for the vegetables. Why on earth do vegetables need a bed? Earth yes, but a bed, now that's just really silly.

Anyway would you start to build me a kennel because I am coming to live with you, I can't take much more of these two.

Though now I'm thinking about it you told me you were having problems with your teeth, in fact you said you were sick to the back teeth of them, yet it's your front teeth that is the problem, so you're as daft as your sister, so I might as well just stay here.

I'm just going to go and see Paul, he is laying slabs in the back garden and as my kennel is virtually next to him, I'll remind him about my carpet. Strike whilst the iron is hot as Gwen says, another stupid saying, nearly as bad as "You could fall in a muck heap and come up smelling of Roses" explain that one??

Going to the post, bye
HRH Traigh

The summer came and went as quickly as before, soon the children were out in coats and scarves but still playing out whatever the weather. We were lucky to be a good distance away from the road and even the little ones were safe. The older children always looked out for the young ones and games involved all ages.

I decided to buy Traigh a coat with him having a thick fur it took ages to dry him after a walk. I bought him a black coat and now I only had to dry his legs and head, I wondered why I hadn't bought one years ago.

Chapter 29

Hello,

Last Saturday it was bonfire night and so Jet and Duracell were put in the far field away from the fireworks, completely unnecessary as they are rather dim, in fact as thick as two short planks, another one of your daft sayings.

Gwen stayed inside with me because I have to say that although I am a big tough guy I don't like fireworks and truth be known neither does Gwen. We played ball (not normally allowed in the house) anyway I caught this rolling ball and broke a tooth. It really made me jump, but I'm a big strong boy and I wanted to carry on playing as it would take Gwen's mind off the fireworks, but she said no, we played a different game and the fireworks were soon over so all was well.

Well, sort of. Gwen took me to the vets to get my mouth checked and he thought there might be some root left in so I had to have that tooth out and another one which Gwen said was probably due to me lifting stones out of the river. I thought that was a bit rich, she threw the ball that did the damage in the first place.

I went back the next day and they gave me a little injection and I was soon asleep, I had the two teeth removed and the rest cleaned. They didn't have enough cages so they let me come round in their office, I was made such a fuss of, it was nice but really I just wanted to have a nap. By the end of the day I was so tired of being fussed over and told how beautiful I was (completely understandable) I just wanted to go home and was glad when Paul came to collect me.

Gwen has removed all my toys for now as she doesn't want the children throwing them for me and I am eating chicken and rice for a few days until my gums heal, I am going to play on it a bit as the chicken is really tasty, I'll spin it out as long as I can.

It's rutting season and I can't sleep for the noise the deer make, they are in the front field and disturbing my nights. I think I should try cotton wool in my ears, Gwen uses it when it's windy to stop her getting earache, I bet it would deaden the racket they make.

Now when my two, who this week I re-named Dipsy and Lala, no don't ask, are coming down to England to see family. I am going to the kennels and I am having my hair done. Actually it's because as soon as they come back we are going up to Ardnamurchan for a week and she doesn't want me to smell of the kennels, so on the Friday I am having a shampoo and my hair just thinned out a bit. Never thought I would have a cut and blow dry.

Don't ring me on Sunday night as 'I'm a Celebrity...Get Me Out of Here' starts. I love watching them try to eat bugs and things, I don't know why they make such a fuss, they should try Gwen's cooking, the bugs would be like caviar.

Must go, I need my beauty sleep, bye for now.
HRH Traigh

We found it hard to believe that another year would soon be upon us, we went on holiday and Traigh as usual went to the kennels. He always walked in without even a glance back and whilst we thought about him, we never worried about him, so we could always enjoy our holiday.

When we collected him, he was always really happy to see us but he literally took seconds to settle down and back to his routine. We often heard of dogs sulking for days if they were left, but he never did, he was just his usual 'laid back Traigh'.

Chapter 30

Hello again,

Did you get anything nice for Xmas? I got a couple of new toys, by the way thanks for the Advent Calendar again, Gwen won't buy me one, she says they are a waste of money, she's just tight.

Paul and I are busy in the garden again, the ground is very hard but he can do some decking. I am keeping a close eye on him, I don't want it to look wonky. He is building a (I bet you can guess) a bar-b-que, the blacksmith at Sandbank has made the grill bit for it. I've seen the plans, well the sketches that he did on the back of a birthday card, it does look good but as you already know, I just don't get the concept of having a barby.

Last evening Paul and I sat out round the chimenea, it was very cold and the sky was full of stars. Paul got well wrapped up but I was fine, I just don't feel the cold.

Anyway we just had a chat like we do, and we escaped the music (if you can call it music) that Gwen was listening to. No wonder she has bad ears listening to that rubbish, she says its heavy metal, she's right, it's like listening to someone banging dustbins lids together. No surprise she's going deaf.

This morning Gwen and I went into the front field for a game of football but football is not the right description at all, she throws it, I fetch it. It is much better than her kicking it, it only ever goes a metre or two, but it should be called throwball. I don't ever take it right back to her, I drop it about three metres away, it just makes me feel better knowing she has to walk a bit.

Lazy bones, anyway I'm trying to help her, she might just loose a bit of weight, you never know.

As you know, of course you do, he's your son, its Nick's 40th birthday soon and Gwen and I are going to write him a poem. Actually she has been a bit mean, she has bought him some nose clippers, she says when you get older, hair grows out of your nose and ears, but I don't see the problem mine does anyway.

Now I didn't want to do a sarcastic poem but Gwen did and after much discussion, she won, she said it was payback time for all the insults she gets from Nick, have you heard the way they talk to each other on the phone? The pair of them are quite mad all they ever do is insult each other.

Once written she is going to send it to you so you can take it to the pub for him and he can open it there and read out his poem. Told you she was mean. You'll want to know what we put, so here it is………….

I'll get Gwen to wrap the pressy and get it in the post asap.

Take care,
HRH Traigh

A little ode to growing old!

Tinker, tailor, soldier, spy,
Never ever tell a lie.
Hair will grow out of your ears,
Until the day you die.

They appear overnight,
And try as you might,
They will not disappear,
But never mind, don't shed a tear.

For you can get out the tweezers,
Join terry's old geezers, and listen to radio 2.
But take my advice and use this device
And tell folk you're just 32.

**Lots of love (really),
Auntie Why.**

Nick and I have always been quite close, as a toddler he called me Aunty Why. Why? No one has a clue, sometimes he still does. When Guy was born he looked just like his cousin at the same age and even now looking at photos when they are both small it's hard to tell them apart.

Nick's nickname at school was tinker, because his last name is Taylor.

They have very different characters, Guy will just do things, Nick will make up his mind what he is doing then, at the very last minute do something completely different.

Chapter 31

Dear Sue and Geoff,

I do hope Nick wasn't too offended with the poem, it wasn't me really, it was the boss. She just looked at me for approval and I couldn't disappoint her now, could I?

Paul needs to wear his glasses more, when you sent a text the other day, you always end with S & G, but Paul looked and said "who's 9 & 5", I can understand the 5 looking like an S, but not a 9 like a G, so he definitely needs his glasses. Anyway he now refers to you as 9&5.

Paul and I have started walking the length of the Loch every other day. We get up really early and Gwen drives us to Glenbranter and we walk back, the shorter walk is 9 miles and the path is beside the Loch and we end up at Benmore, the other side takes you up into the hills before you drop back down toward the Loch and is 12 miles. Paul takes his camera and has taken some great views, if I smell a deer, I lay down straightaway and Paul can often then get a good picture.

We stop about half way so Paul can have a coffee (and a rest) I just have a drink of water and Paul will wait for me whilst I have a swim. If I ask nicely he throws me a stick and I will swim out to fetch it for him. It keeps him amused.

Gwen will often stop and do a bit of fishing once she's dropped us off. It saves me having to go with her, as I do find it quite boring.

Will write again soon,
HRH Traigh

If Paul and Traigh walked the shorter walk I would often see them from the opposite side of the Loch and would give them a ring. I would always get home before them and have breakfast on the go. Paul would have a quick shower, breakfast and out to work by 8.00am.

Traigh was always a big dog but this walking was building his muscles and when you stroked him, he was solid.

This walking went on until late autumn and it was just too dark in the morning, slowly the walks got shorter as daybreak became later. Eventually his morning walks were with me at least until the following spring.

Towards the end of the year we had snow and Traigh was in his element, he loved it.

Chapter 32

Dear Sue and Geoff,

Paul and I have taken to walking Pucks Glen, there are some amazingly tall trees, it's a lovely walk.

There is a little girl on the Park, she is only tiny and when she walks Pucks Glen with her daddy, she takes up a fairy and hides it. I think she rides on his shoulders most of the time. The next time they go, if it has disappeared she knows the other fairies have made a new friend and it has gone to live with them. I often look as well, but as yet I haven't seen one.

Spring is in the air and the birds are singing. The swallows are back and are busy building their nests. We have one just above the kitchen window and it's funny to see Gwen jump as they swoop up towards their nest, she thinks they are going to crash into the window, she actually ducks. Why do you have one word that means two or three different things? Like ducks?

The front field is full of red deer, they are even happily grazing there in the middle of the day. They seem to have absolutely no fear. I give them a very wide berth, they are much bigger than me. We did have a deer that was very grey, so we presumed it was very old. It moved very slowly and had started to limp a little, so we think it must have died over the last winter. It was so slow it was the only one I wasn't frightened of. Gwen had called it White Face.

I think you should suggest that my two both go to Spec Savers. We were going to Ardentinny for a walk and a picnic and they didn't see a Submarine (which was enormous) in the water, they must be blind. As you know the road runs alongside the Loch. Paul said he didn't see it as he was

driving, okay I can buy that, but Gwen missed it completely.
When we got to the beach I pointed it out to them and I know
they felt pretty stupid and I felt pretty good, I can tell you.
One up to me!
   I must go now, I really do have a lot to do.

Take care,
HRH Traigh

So far it had been a pretty good year, we had now been at Stratheck for 2 years and people were getting to know us.

In the December Paul and I went on holiday and whilst away had a phone call from Guy to say that he had become a daddy. Guy and his partner had become proud parents to a little boy who they named Alfie, we were absolutely delighted. We were looking forward to the family coming up for New Year. Sophie was now growing up and Alfie was 3 weeks old.

Chapter 33

Dear Sue and Geoff,

Yippee, it'll soon be Christmas!

What's your weather like? Up here it's freezing. I don't mind but Gwen does and she's got on so many clothes she's round. It takes her so long to take them off when she goes for lunch that she has hardly time to eat before it's time to put them all back on again.

They have bought new thermals to keep themselves warm and yet again I don't understand as thermals are what the weather girl talks about when she's pointing at her map on the telly.

The river is really high and fast flowing, I am not allowed near it as Paul says I would be swept away, confusion again, I thought that was a brush.

Part of the bank has collapsed which had the Sandmartins nests, so I don't know if they will attempt to build again. We always thought we were lucky to have them here, Gwen wonders if they go much further north.

Gwen's away soon to the caravan show in Glasgow for four days, so Paul and I will have some peace, can't wait. The other bonus is that the Cricket season has not started so I won't have to put up with Paul wanting to watch that, thank goodness. It's the slowest game there is along with golf. It would be better if they moved those three little sticks out of the way. It will be nice for the two of us to have some time on our own.

Oh well, back to work.
HRH Traigh

Whilst I was at the caravan show a friend asked how Traigh was, I replied, "He's fine thanks, best dog in the world," to which Keith replied, "I'll second that." I could not have been more proud.

Whilst the family have the holiday parks they are also sheep farmers and understand what an asset a good sheepdog can be.

We always found that people would always ask how Traigh was before they asked after us.

Chapter 34

Hello again, are you both well?

We have all been to the beach today and Paul and I were swimming and having a great time, Gwen shouted to us and Paul didn't hear, I did but pretended I hadn't, after a while Paul noticed Gwen trying to get his attention, he swam back to the shore and Gwen pointed out 'wobbly things' floating in the water. They were jellyfish, thousands of them (no I'm not exaggerating).

Well, that was the end of our swimming, Paul said they were probably harmless, but we decided not to risk it, so we played in the rock pools instead. We went for a walk so I could dry off a bit and then had a picnic, at least they did. I have two meals a day and I don't snack in between, it's not good for you.

A couple of the dogs that come to the park must eat the wrong food or are just greedy, they are massive, I have said they need to take more exercise, but they just take no notice and then go back to sleep. It is a shame as every walk I go on is so different, they really are missing out. I could ask Gwen to talk to their humans but she may not be diplomatic enough, you know what she's like.

I hear you are both coming up soon, I'll try to book some nice weather, Gwen suggests taking you to up to Loch Etive, which is on the way to Fort William. We go there quite a lot, it is so peaceful and the scenery is stunning. We can either have a picnic at Etive or go on up to Fort William for lunch, let's see what the weather is shall we?

Oh and by the way, I've got a new duvet in the back of my truck, Gwen said the old one was past it, past what? I'm getting impressed with her, she disinfected the back of my

*truck and then hosed it out and even had the common sense
to let it dry, I tell you my training methods are doing just
fine.*

*Will write again soon,
HRH Traigh*

We did go to Loch Etive and my Sister hoped we would
see some deer. The sign at the top of the Glen says 5 miles
but there is a 1 missing, it's 15.

We rounded a corner on the long single-track road that
takes you down the glen and was surrounded by about 60 red
deer. They were going nowhere fast, we sat for ages just
watching them and my sister took lots of photos, it made her
day.

Chapter 35

Hello,

It's that time of year again, the deer in the front field are keeping me awake, it's like trying to sleep through lions roaring. Gwen often has cotton wool in her ears for the earache so she doesn't always hear them.

Paul sometimes gets up in the night because of the noise so we watch a film, but he's a bit mean, he never lets me choose. I sometimes just go back to bed because he watches re-runs of cricket. My friend Jean next door calls it "that silly game of bat and ball", it usually gets her into trouble, she loves stirring it.

Jean is one of my best friends, she won't mind me saying she is a pensioner, let's say her body is slowing down a bit, but believe me her mind is not, she's just wicked, I love her. Jean and Paul are always poking fun at each other and insult each other on a daily basis. Now Jean also has posh initials, but Jeans are after her name and she has MBE, whereas mine are before, my lovely HRH. Jean's husband Bert says the MBE stands for More Blinking Expense. Actually he didn't say blinking.

It's not bad weather for the time of year but the days are getting shorter. Paul says it's a bit too mild for this time of year and we'll pay for it later. Sorry but once again I don't get it, what will we pay for?

Talk again soon,
HRH Traigh

Traigh is right, Jean and Bert are both quite mad, but lovely. Jean loves Traigh and he knows it.

Paul made Traigh two boards to lie on that he covered in Astroturf, one which was just inside the garden gate and the other at the side of the fence between Jean and our back garden.

Traigh has never barked a lot but he got Jeans attention by making a funny squeak and she would then take him into the front field for a while.

Chapter 36

Dear Sue and Geoff,

It's been snowing heavily this week and the temperature is dropping. Paul and I had to dig out the drive. We used the tractor to move most of it, but then we had to dig with spades as the tractor would have ripped up the tarmac. As you know it's a long drive and it seemed to take forever.

We eventually gave up as it was snowing so much that it was covering up what we had already moved and we were getting nowhere. There were very few folk on the Park but Gwen went to see if they were all okay and if they needed any milk or anything fetching but most of them said they were going home whilst they could get out.

Gwen went and got some groceries and stocked up more than normal. When she came back we went into the front field and I disappeared under the snow. I was tunnelling under the soft snow and it was good fun. The snow came over the top of Gwen's wellies and she would have been better wearing her waders.

It's now minus 17, my goodness it's really cold. There is hardly any traffic moving, it's as if the world has stopped.

We have decided to work inside and give the clubhouse a good clean before the New Year. I have been allowed inside, Gwen took one of my big towels in and I had to lie on that. I have never been in the clubhouse before, it's really nice.

Paul put the TV on so we could listen to some music, but unfortunately Gwen thinks she can sing, she can't, she is really bad and Paul must think so too because he turned the TV over, but he put on a programme about holidays, all sun and sea, not a good idea when it's so cold just breathing in hurts. I don't think Gwen was impressed.

I'm going to say goodbye now and ask to go out again, I want to play, this snow is brilliant, I'm just loving it.

Take care,
HRH Traigh

The snow and freezing temperature seemed to go on for a long time. I slipped on the balcony and ripped a tendon in my shoulder and it was very sore. I then bought some grips that go over your footwear. If only I had bought them before the bad weather. I put them onto a pair of boots and would recommend them to anyone. I have used them every winter since and they are brilliant.

Chapter 37

Hello again.

Well after that cold winter it looks as if spring is arriving. It's still a bit cold but the sun is shining and Gwen says the bulbs are showing through.

This year we are going to have a fun day and hope to also raise some money for the Clic Sargent Children's cancer charity. Our friends Chris and Kim's daughter is in remission from cancer and they are doing lots of different events to raise money.

They say that Clic helped all the family so much and held them together through some very difficult times, so it's their way of saying thank you. I shall be proud to help.

Gwen and I are back in our routine of going fishing, but I do have to get up so early. I watch from a safe distance and always to her left as she casts with her right hand, I don't want to get hooked if you know what I mean. It's a bit boring but Gwen enjoys it. On Tuesday we were out and I was laid down watching quietly when a little roe deer came quite close and took a drink from the Loch, it was lovely to see as it was so near and didn't seem at all frightened of me, it probably knew I wouldn't hurt it.

Paul is busy grass cutting and he is going to put a pitch and put in the front field. One of the young lads on the park had asked if this could be done and Paul said, "Yes, but come and help me." I think it's great if the youngsters get involved.

The pair of them are out there now putting down 6 holes and Jean is going to make the flags. I think it will get used a lot.

Anyway, must go and supervise,
HRH Traigh

The golf was a great success and was used by all ages, including us, although I am not very good and Paul beats me every time, but it is good fun.

Traigh comes round with us and always waits to be told when he can follow us to the next hole. He's also pretty useful helping me find the ball when I hit the ball into the long grass, which is pretty often.

There is often a knock at the door early evening and it's one of the teenagers asking if Paul wants to play golf. Of course Traigh goes too!

Chapter 38

Hello, hope you are both doing fine.

We had the Stratheck Fun day on Saturday, very hard work and brilliant fun. The setting up was done on Friday and by early evening we were all shattered.

We had tombolas, raffles, various stalls, burgers etc.... in the afternoon they did a tug of war, it was funny. One team waited until they were pulling hard and then all let go at the same time, the other team all fell in a heap on the floor.

There was also a truck pull, Gwen just cannot see the point of pulling a truck when it's got an engine, she has absolutely no sense of humour. Loads of people had a go and it looked really hard to do. When the last person had done, Gwen jumped in and drove it instead, it made her day as she loves big vehicles and nice cars.

Paul has no interest in cars at all, as long as it gets him from A to B he couldn't care less what he drives. I think Gwen should have been born a man, she hates shopping, likes football and fishing and positively drools over classic cars. Her favourite is a series three E-Type roadster, but take my advice, don't ask her about it or she'll bore you to tears.

We raised quite a bit of money and decided to do it all again next year. We all learnt a lot and next year should be even better.

After taking down all the marquees on Sunday the field looked bare.

We decided to have an easy day on Thursday (our day off) and we just went to Jubilee Point about 6 miles up the road. My two had a picnic and I had a swim. Paul decided to

be a wuss and only had a bit of a paddle. I think he must be
going soft as he gets older, he said it was cold, what a wimp.
Gwen says you are coming up soon, so I'll see you then.
HRH Traigh

All the hard work for the fun day was worth it as lots of owners said it was a great day and for us that's what it is all about. People that work hard all week deserve to have some quality time at the weekend that's relaxing.

If you need to relax, you need to visit Argyll, it's stunning, put it on a list of things to do, you won't regret it.

Chapter 39

Dear Sue and Geoff,

Paul was going to Dunoon and saw a cat at the top of the road, unfortunately it had been run over, but he realised it must have had kittens. Amazingly Gwen saw them playing by the roadside a couple of days later.

Gwen caught one of them straight away and took it to Jean and asked her to keep it until she came back. Gwen managed to get another one and put it in the bath, obviously without water. The third one had vanished. Gwen rang the SSPCA who came out the next day to collect them, but she only took one, there was no way Jean and Bert were parting with their tiny kitten.

Bert has decided to call him Innit, he's a nice little thing. He's getting spoilt rotten. He has started chasing things so Gwen hopes he will be a good mouser.

When Jean goes for a walk he follows on behind, it takes her ages as he is just so tiny (and so are his legs) he is like her shadow.

The Park is looking great, the golf is going down a storm (another of your funny sayings) and the plants are blooming and full of colour.

Paul and Gwen have planted clematis around the skip area, I hope it's as successful as it was at St Catherine's. The clematis at St Catherine's gets better every year. It looks so much better than looking at the skip.

I said they both planted them, in fact it was Gwen, Paul would have put them upside down. I have to say it does look nice.

Will write again soon,
HRH Traigh

It was turning out to be another good summer, the weather was not as good as the previous year but it never seems to make any difference to anyone. Our second Granddaughter Layla was born at the beginning of August, so now we had three Grandchildren, Sophie, Alfie and now Layla, as they were all happy and healthy we felt very lucky.

Chapter 40

Dear Sue and Geoff,

August has been a busy month, that's why I have not written, I've just been so busy.

Paul's sister Karen and family came up along with Paul's mum. It was Aaron's 16ᵗʰ birthday on the Thursday and we had a great day.

First of all we went to Blairmore, so they could all have a go at fishing off the end of the pier, then down to the beach at Ardentinny. We all collected large stones and built a raised area to put all the disposable barbys on.

Then we played games like boules and football, I couldn't play boules as I can't throw, but I did play football, I'm pretty good at it. I'm surprised the Scotland team haven't talent scouted me. I also went swimming whilst they ate their lunch. The games were all played again and then we packed up to come home. It took ages to collect water to put out the barbys before we put them in the bin.

We had another go at fishing on the way back.

We arrived home and then all went out to play golf, even Gwen. I stayed with Gwen all the way round as she was always last and I felt duty bound to stay with her. We played for quite a long time.

On the way to the very last hole everyone was waiting for Gwen as usual, she hit the ball pretty hard (for her) and it went half way across the field (or fairway). We walked over to the ball and she used her hand signal to ask me to sit and stay, so I did. Then she hit the ball again and it landed on the green, it was just luck, trust me, she has no talent for the game at all. It was amazing.

The game ended and everyone went home, except me. Gwen had forgotten to tell me to follow her so I stayed where I was. After about 45minutes Gwen realised what she had done, or hadn't done and came out to fetch me, she had the good grace to apologise profusely and she felt really bad, I could have made her feel worse by ignoring her, but it's not my style.

To top it off, I didn't even get any birthday cake!

Will write again soon,
HRH Traigh

It was a great day, all together having fun, I took lots of photos and Traigh seems to be in every one.

Chapter 41

Dear Sue and Geoff,

Paul and Gwen are going back to Egypt so I'm off to the kennels again, I thought I had better write before I go.

Gwen has to go and have her ear looked at again, she's getting a lot of earache, can't be very nice and I must be getting soft in my old age as even I have sympathy for old bossy boots.

I had to go to the vets for my annual check-up and my ears were just fine but I have to have my teeth cleaned again. It's no problem, I don't mind, all the staff are really friendly. One of the nurses is actually called Gwen.

I have to tell you the story my pal told me last week, it's about his human friend.

This lady lives down south and just before Christmas she went to London to do some shopping. After a while she was ready for a break so decided to go in to one of the large department stores for a coffee.

Now she got her coffee and a KitKat and went to find a table, it was really busy but she managed to find a seat. A few moments later a man arrived with his coffee and a muffin and asked if he could sit opposite her.

They exchanged a couple of words as to how busy it was.

She broke off a piece of KitKat and started to eat it, then he broke a piece off, she didn't know what to do, she didn't want to make a fuss as it was so busy and after all it was only a KitKat, she ate another piece and he ate the last one. She decided the best thing to do was just leave. As she stood up she was suddenly really angry, she gathered her bags and then leant over the table and broke off half of his muffin and stormed out, in disgust she threw the half muffin in a bin.

Before she got to the railway station she went into one more store, she went to pay for her goods, opened her handbag and there was her KitKat.

I can tell you, I laughed and laughed. It's just the sort of thing that would happen to Gwen, but I promise you, it wasn't her.

Take care,
HRH Traigh

I promise it wasn't me too.

Chapter 42

Dear Sue and Geoff,

It was a fun day again on Saturday and again it was really good. There were a few more stalls and even a candyfloss machine, although why folks want to eat that stuff I have no idea. It looks awful and it's pink, not one of my favourite colours.

Chris and Kim with friends have started The Brianne Roberts Trust which will help families who have youngsters with cancer, there are still great amounts given to Clic Sargent as well.

There was a race night in the clubhouse in the evening and that raised quite a bit for the charity. I could hear the cheering as folks shouted their chosen horses over the finishing line.

On Sunday morning I helped them take down the marquees and pack everything away. I can't believe a year has passed since the last one, I suppose it's true, time does go quickly when you are having fun.

It will be time for the children's summer holidays soon and I get lots of attention. I have them all well trained to throw my ball for me and then I pass it back to them through the gate. If they are really tiny children I pass it through a small gap in the fence, it's easier for them. They know when I have had enough, I just say thank you and goodbye and go inside for a rest.

I am slowing down a bit, I can't manage to play for as long as I used to and I am finding it a bit harder to get going in the morning. I used to laugh (to myself) when Gwen said she was creaking in a morning, I now know what she meant.

I need to go now, Paul and I are working on the riverside path cutting back the brambles, actually Paul's going to cut them back, I am going for a swim, although I haven't told him yet.

Take care,
HRH Traigh

We had noticed Traigh had slowed down a little bit, he still liked to play, but not with as much energy as before, although he was still in the river or the Loch every day. I have never known a sheepdog who liked water as much as him.

I'm glad to say I only had to tap my leg and call his name for him to swim back to me and get out of the water. I would then ask him to stay whilst I walked a few metres away so he would shake himself and not wet me through.

Chapter 43

Hello again.

Now where has this year gone, can you believe it's nearly Christmas again.

My two have bought a 3D TV, well Paul has. Gwen thinks it's a waste of money as the other TV is just fine. If you watch the 3D programmes you have to put on these strange glasses.

The first programme we watched was a programme about a coral reef and the fish looked as if they were swimming out of the TV. Well, that's what they said I couldn't see a thing it was all blurry because they didn't give me a pair of glasses.

Gwen doesn't really like it, I think it's because she already wears glasses, so she's wearing glasses on top of glasses.

I walked into the side of the sofa the other day, I just didn't see it, I was glad no one saw me, I felt an idiot. I also can't get down the steps into the garden as easily on a night, I must ask Paul to put a bigger bulb in the outside light, this getting older really is a bit of a pain.

Gwen's sent her Christmas cards already, she started writing them months ago, I'm not kidding, it's a job she hates doing and if it was left to Paul then no one would get one at all. Paul is like Guy when it comes to cards, neither of them think it is right to chop down a rainforest just to send cards.

We are decorating this evening, well Christmas decorations anyway. Paul and I will do it, Gwen doesn't like Christmas as you know, she's a 'bar humbug', and apparently Paul says your Nick is too.

Will write again soon, have a nice Christmas.
HRH Traigh

Christmas and New Year once again was a nice affair although it is true I'm not a great fan.

Everything seemed just fine and then on the Tuesday after New Year we had one really bad day.

Chapter 44

Hi,

Sorry not to have written before but things have been rather hectic.

Monday evening a storm was brewing, some folk had already gone home as they were back at work the following day. During the night it got worse, all three of us got up really early.

I am not going to go into great detail as it is too upsetting, but we had people injured and needed the help of the emergency services, who were excellent.

At one point we had thirty some folk in the house, four dogs, two cats, a budgie and lots of paramedics. To make matters worse the electric went off and the gas had to be turned off for safety reasons.

The Police said that everyone had to be evacuated, except for us, so all these folk drove or were driven by Gwen down to Hunters Quay Holiday Village where they were all given caravans or lodges to stay in and were fed and watered. The staff down there did a fantastic job for which we were very grateful.

When it calmed down we went and looked at the mess Mother Nature had caused and what a mess she had made.

It's been an awful week and I'm glad they don't have to cook my food, Gwen and Paul have been managing with a camping stove and candles. I would have liked to go to Hunters Quay with everybody else, but the police said we had to stay and you can't argue with the boys in blue.

Clearing up is being done now and that is giving them something to do, I wish I could help more, they are both awfully quiet which is worrying me.

Anyway, you two look after yourselves,
HRH Traigh

It was a day we won't forget, the wind speed was terrifying, but there were folk out there that needed help. A couple of people on the Park were really terrific and also put themselves in danger to help others.

This terrible day pulled everyone together and Stratheck became even more of a community.

Chapter 45

Hi,

Things are settling down now and we are getting sorted out. The park is starting to look good again.

I went to the vets to have my annual check over and she said my eyes were getting a bit cloudy and asked Gwen to keep an eye on them which I thought was a silly thing to say, but other than that I'm fine.

I have to say I cannot see just as good as I did, especially on a night and I don't like going out just before bedtime but I don't want to make a fuss.

Paul and Gwen have noticed me bumping into things so I have had to go to the vets again and she said I probably had cataracts on both eyes and she has referred me to the Veterinary Hospital in Glasgow. It's a teaching hospital.

If you remember I don't like Glasgow very much and this Hospital is at a place called Bearsden, the very name is scary enough. I don't think I am going to like this at all.

Gwen's bought me this extender lead that I have to wear when I go out at night. Paul and I walk round the boatyard and along the front field and if I am going to bump into something he can give it a quick pull and I stop before I hit anything. I thought it was a bit stupid at first but I now realise that without it I would be covered in bruises.

We are just waiting for the appointment to come in the post, Gwen and Paul have tried to tell me not to worry, but I can tell you it's a bit difficult as I don't know what they are going to do.

I'll keep you informed,
HRH Traigh

We were very concerned as to the outcome of Traigh's eye condition as we didn't know of any person with cataracts let alone an animal.

We were desperate for the appointment to come through, just watching him try to get about the house was awful. We moved coffee tables and other items out of his way and made sure doors were always closed so he didn't walk into them.

He couldn't see any of his toys unless they were absolutely under his nose. We got him a bright luminous pink ball and if we were fairly close to him we could pass him this and he would push it back towards us with his nose. Paul and I would take it in turns to play this for hours in the evening.

Chapter 46

Hi,

I've been for my appointment, it wasn't too bad. I had to stand on a table and this nice man called George looked in my eyes with lots of different types of lights, sometimes he turned the ceiling lights out and looked into my eyes in the dark.

He put me some eye drops in too, but I don't know why, maybe it's just fashionable.

After a while I got bored as he was asking my two loads of questions about me, it was a bit rude talking over me like that, but he was nice, anyway I asked to be lifted down and then went and laid down until they had done.

We came home and it appears I have to go to the hospital and I will be there from Monday morning until Wednesday evening, the down side is I can't have anything to eat after 6.00pm on the Sunday. That bits not good, I love my dinner.

It's a short letter, but all this unrest is making me tired, I'm away to my bed.

HRH Traigh

Soon we were on our way to the Veterinary Hospital early on the Monday, we were halfway along the Loch when Paul put into words what we had both been thinking. What if it didn't work? We were so worried as he just didn't have enough quality of life.

We decided that if they could not restore his eyesight that we would ask them to put Traigh to sleep whilst he was

112

under the anaesthetic and use any of his organs that could help other dogs. It seemed to take ages to get there.

We reluctantly and bravely said our goodbye to him, even though we knew we were leaving him in safe hands and we came home and waited for the phone call which we were expecting around teatime. We tried to work but we found it so hard to concentrate. The phone call arrived sooner than we thought, but I'll let Traigh tell you.

Chapter 47

Dear Geoff and Sue,

I've had my cataracts removed.

A nurse shaved my leg and gave me an injection and pretty soon I was feeling sleepy. What happened next? I don't know, I woke up and I could see, it was a bit blurry to start with, but I can see again.

People kept coming to have a look at me and asked if I was okay, they were very concerned and caring, really kind, so I have decided to book old bossy boots in for a few lessons.

They keep putting drops in my eyes, I don't like it much, but I'm not making a fuss, if Gwen were here she would be saying "keep still, it's good for you" so even though she's not, I had better still do as she would tell me. I'm being made quite a fuss of.

I must have slept a lot because it didn't seem long before my two came to collect me. They were informed that I was a perfect patient and hadn't made any fuss at all, even when I came round (round what?), I just sat there quietly. I could see they were very proud of me. They said, "Yes, they knew I was just brilliant." It's taken them a long time to agree with my mother, but hey, every dog has its day!

We came home with such a lot of tablets and eye drops, I hope my two know what they are doing. I also have to go back next week for a check-up.

Also in my last letter I forgot to tell you, Gwen bought Paul a ticket for the sea plane for his birthday, I don't know why I didn't remember before, anyway I'm glad I'm not going I wouldn't like it, Gwen's not going either, we'll just wave from the Park if he flies over here.

Will write soon, now I can see better.
HRH Traigh

We were so relieved that he had come through the operation and although knew there were no promises the signs were looking good.

The first night he was home we could tell he was uncomfortable, he never made a noise but we just knew. I said I would stay with him but Paul wanted to stay with him so he put a quilt on the floor near him and stayed with him all night, I couldn't sleep and kept getting up to see if he was okay and in the end I just stayed up too and the next morning he looked much better.

We had to make out a chart for all his tablets and drops as we didn't want to double up or miss out on any of his medication.

We made a chart with the times of day and which medication he was to have and whoever gave him his drops or tablets would highlight that time, so either of us could glance and know where we were up to in the day.

George had asked us to give him a small treat after his eye drops as most dogs would object and a treat would make it easier.

Traigh pretty soon cottoned on to this and when it was time for his drops he would come and sit with his head up, he never ever made a fuss. He was as we had said at the hospital, just brilliant.

He had to wear a plastic collar so he didn't rub his eyes and again he took it all in his stride.

Chapter 48

Hi again,

Well it seems I'm having these drops for a while yet, they start early in the morning and then I have them every two hours until 10.00pm, sometime it's three sets of drops with 15 minutes in between them, no wonder they need the chart. I'm still on tablets too only I don't get a treat with them. My pals say they get them wrapped up in a bit of ham, no chance of that here with Gwen, I just get them put in my mouth and I have to swallow them, and after them being so good I wouldn't spit them out, it would be so ungrateful.

I went for my check-up and the drops will get less as time goes on, but one of them I will always have to have, but it will eventually end up just once a day. So the treats would have been on the decline anyway. I also have thought, I only used to get one treat but I have two eyes so they should have given me two treats.

I hadn't realised until I saw Gwen get me a treat, it's not a treat at all, it's just one of the tiny biscuits that I would be having for my breakfast or dinner anyway. What a cheat, I thought I was getting something special. I thought they tasted familiar. I ought to know better I suppose.

Right I'm away, Paul and I are going for a walk, I'm not allowed to run about yet, something to do with pressure.

Bye for now,
HRH Traigh

It was so good to have him home and on the mend, we felt like we had won the lottery. He had lots of visits to see George and usually Paul took him, as he wasn't allowed to jump up into the truck and with him being a big dog I just couldn't lift him.

Chapter 49

Hello, how are you?

Paul has finally done his seaplane flight, he's cancelled it twice because of my appointments and on the third time the organisers had to cancel because of the weather. So it was fourth time lucky.

Gwen and I went into the front field and waved as the plane went over, unfortunately he didn't see us as he was sitting at the other side looking towards the Massan, but he said it was a great experience and would love to do it again. We looked at his photos and they are really good. I'll show you next time you are here.

I've got an upset tummy, the vet says it is colitis. I have tablets to take but I don't feel very well and I like to keep active but I'm just too tired and my tummy is sore, it's back to the chicken and rice which is the only bonus.

This colitis could be because I have had my eyes done and it was the shock of being able to see again.

I was sneakily listening in to Paul and Gwen saying that if I was human they could have explained what would happen regarding the operation and recovery and it wouldn't have been such a shock. They could have tried, I would have listened.

Because I am really tired I have asked my two if I can go on more walks but just little ones. It's okay they have agreed, I go out often then I have a sleep.

Pauls bought Gwen a guitar, now this he will regret, seeing as she can't sing, can't whistle, can't even hum in tune what's the chance of her being able to play? I can tell you truthfully its zero, I've heard her and she's rubbish, she may be the one with bad ears but it's me that's got the earache. Fighting cats sound better.

Gwen says I don't have to listen to her I can go in another room, doesn't work, she's got an amplifier. I keep trying to distract her so she'll put the thing down, I'm just hoping she'll break a string, SOON. There isn't a music shop in Dunoon so she would have to wait until they went over the water to replace it, please don't offer to post one up if she asks.

Okay time to go and ask Paul to take me for a walk, he's so obedient, I'm rather proud of him.

Bye
HRH Traigh

Winter was upon us again and Traigh had really slowed down and although he looked good we were keeping an eye on him. We didn't want to think he was getting old, but he was a big dog and he wasn't going to go on forever, always our thoughts were for his quality of life and our wants had to be second. We just wanted him to live forever and be active, something that just doesn't happen.

Chapter 50

Hi,

Guess what? After Christmas we are moving to Loch Eck Caravan Park, it's a lot smaller. I think head office thinks Gwen's getting on a bit and needs it easier. The cottage is alright, but I'm going to miss my pals, especially Cooper. It's not as if they can visit on their own, its only one and a half miles up the road but of course there is no pavement and it can be quite a fast road.

We have started to clear things out and are giving it to charity. The Brianne Roberts Trust of course. It's really hard knowing what to keep. I feel really sorry for them as they are getting rid of things they want to keep but just won't have the room.

Unfortunately there is no garden, there is a balcony, but nowhere for Gwen to grow her vegetables or have fruit trees, let alone a greenhouse and a grapevine.

There are boxes everywhere, I have given away a lot of my toys, I don't play with them anymore so they might as well go, I'd only be keeping them for sentimental reasons, but I can now understand why Gwen keeps getting upset when she has to give away things she's had and treasured for years.

Anyway have a nice Christmas, I did remember to ask you not to send me an advent calendar didn't I? I can't have them anymore.

See you in the New Year.
HRH Traigh

This was a very hard time for us, we didn't want to leave Stratheck, it was our home and after a lot of hard work it was a beautiful Park with lovely people. We considered leaving, but Scotland is where we belong so after a lot of thought we decided we should at least try it. So we moved the one and a half miles up the Loch and it was the hardest and most painful move either of us had ever done.

Chapter 51

Hi,

The move was okay, Dipsy and Lala had put my bed under the window in the lounge but I didn't want it there, so eventually they moved it to where I wanted it, well it should be my choice, I don't go and move their bed.

Gwen's trying to fit things in, you take your life in your own hands if you open a cupboard door at the moment, by the time they find everything it will be time for them to retire.

I had to go to the vets for my annual check-up and boosters, Gwen aired her concerns for me as I was not as active as I had been. My heart checked out just fine and I have no lumps or bumps that I shouldn't have. Gwen was reassured that she would know when I had had enough. I didn't like the conversation so I tuned out.

The TV signal is really poor and it's like watching a programme through a snowstorm, we usually have to turn it off and listen to music instead, that's okay if Paul or I choose otherwise it's that head banging stuff.

Gwen's been to the caravan show again for four days and she bought me a new bed, funny I thought they sold caravans. It's brown and squashy and very comfortable and I soon fall asleep when I lay down.

Paul and I had some time on our own which was nice, we watched DVDs laid on the floor together, Paul really likes being on the dog shelf, he'd rather be on the floor than sit on the sofa.

The Park is quite steep and so the walking is pretty hard, it's showed that neither Gwen or I are fit enough or just getting a bit old, but at least they are going on holiday soon so I'm going to the kennels for a rest, must remind Gwen to get me some more eye drops my bottle is nearly empty.

Well I'll say goodbye for now and go and pack my bag for my holiday. I do hope I am next to a sensible dog and not a wimpy thing.

Bye,
HRH Traigh

Off we went on holiday and enjoyed ourselves and as always thought of Traigh but we were not worried about him at all, he always came back fine.

Chapter 52

Chapter 51 was his last letter. Traigh came home from the kennels and as usual settled back just fine, but over the next few weeks we noticed he didn't have a zest for life anymore. He just wanted to sleep.

One Sunday evening we realised that the awful decision that comes to all animal lovers would have to come sooner than we thought. When he was out walking he was just slightly dragging his back legs, it was only just noticeable but you could just hear his claws scraping the ground.

Monday evening he was very restless so we stayed up with him, in between bouts of restlessness he would fall fast asleep and snore. The next morning he seemed to be okay although tired and didn't really want to go out.

Late Tuesday afternoon he started with his colitis again and during the evening Paul and I made the decision that we had been dreading, it was time to say goodbye. We always said that we would make the decision sooner rather than later when he could be suffering, his welfare had to come first. We stayed up with him all night and rang the vets first thing in the morning.

We both took him and the Veterinary nurse Gwen was there which seemed very apt. Traigh was lifted onto the table and he was given a small injection that very quickly made him fall asleep, we talked to him all the time although I have no idea what we said, the next injection stopped his heart and then he was gone. Traigh was just laid there without movement, our dear friend, just gone!

We all cried, Nurse Gwen was really upset and Paul was inconsolable. I thought the vet would have to administer first aid to him. I have never seen a man so distraught and for once I didn't know how to deal with it.

They left us alone with him for a while and I just wanted him to wake up, we drove home in silence and we realised that now there were only two of us.

Even though we knew what we had done was the right thing, we felt numb and spent the rest of the day in a daze.

The next day was Thursday, our day off, the first one without him. It was a horrible day and there were and still are plenty of bad days. We realise we were so lucky, he was with us for many years and we have such wonderful memories, he really was so special.

I'd like to say life got back to normal, but normal had been having Traigh around and I feel as if we are often both pretending to be okay for the sake of the other. It has to get better and I'm sure in time it will.

In all the time we were together he never had a smack and we never needed to raise our voice to him, he was absolutely one in a million, the best friend we ever had.

Thank you for reading this book and I hope you have a friend like we had.

After a while I wrote this poem.

Traigh

We turn round to him but he's no longer there,
We're wrapped up in sadness we can't seem to share.
We feel so alone, no friend at our side,
But we will remember him with enormous pride.

The sadness will go and the joy will come,
When we remember what the three of us have done.
In time we'll look back, smile and feel glad,
For all the wonderful times that we had.

You took so little, yet you gave so much,
You enhanced our lives and our souls you touched.
So farewell our dear friend, it was time to part,
But forever you will be right here in our heart.

So thanks for the fun and the laughter too,
For all the things we all got to do.
Will we replace you, will we even try,
It was just too hard to say goodbye.

CPSIA information can be obtained
at www.ICGtesting.com
Printed in the USA
BVHW042218100619
550683BV00004B/12/P

9 781528 903639